Space Marine

Extinction Fleet Book 2
By Sean-Michael Argo

Copyright 2017
by Sean-Michael Argo

Space Marine Loki

Extinction Fleet, Volume 2

Sean-Michael Argo

Published by Sean-Michael Argo, 2023.

Also by Sean-Michael Argo

Extinction Fleet
Space Marine Loki
Space Marine Ajax

Starwing Elite
Attack Ships
Alpha Lance

Standalone
War Machines
DinoMechs: Battle Force Jurassic

Edited by TL Bland

Table of Contents

"They have seen my strength for themselves, have watched me rise from the darkness of war, dripping with my enemy's blood. I swam in the blackness of night, hunting monsters and killing them one by one; death was my errand and the fate they had earned." - Beowulf, epic poem, author unknown, circa 700-1000 A.D.

THE HUNGRY DARK

In the half-light, it almost looked human.

And then it moved.

Camouflage was abandoned in an explosive revelation of teeth and claws.

Deputy Stratton screamed as he squeezed the trigger of his sub-machine gun, the weapon kicking wildly in his hands as it spit rounds from its short barrel.

The thing that was not a man ducked low to avoid most of the bullets, scuttling forward on limbs that now ended in pointed blades of hardened chitin. Somewhere behind the creature, in the murky glow of the underground drainage chamber, there was a shriek of pain and anger as the deputy's salvo managed to hit one of the other deputies.

Stratton scampered backwards, still firing, doing his best to track the nightmare with the barrel of his weapon.

"*On your left!*" came the desperate voice of Deputy Marcone. Hearing it, Stratton hurled himself to the right and out of the way.

Marcone rushed into the chamber, emerging from a side tunnel already firing upon the creature. The small caliber rounds didn't damage the thing much individually, but as Marcone continued shooting, the sheer volume of rounds did the job. By the time the deputy's magazine clicked empty Stratton had been able to regain his footing and draw a bead on the wounded monster. Three rapid bursts from his weapon at point-blank range wiped the creature's sickeningly humanoid face from existence. The sight of it, however, was burned permanently into Stratton's mind.

"Where's Bowski?" asked Stratton as he and Marcone rapidly swapped out their empty magazines.

"Bowskiiii..." From the darkness of the drainage chamber

rasped a voice that could not possibly be considered human any longer. from the darkness of the drainage chamber.

4

Marcone saw it before Stratton and raised his sub-machine gun to unleash with full-auto. In the muzzle flash strobe light of Marcone's fury, Stratton caught a brief glimpse of a giant armored form.

It stood nearly seven feet tall, or it would have, had it not been so clearly stooped to avoid scraping its head against the ceiling. Sparks flew as the small caliber rounds were deflected by the unknown enemy's armor. Stratton raised his weapon to fire just as the armored assailant launched its own counterattack.

In an eyeblink, the enemy leapt from its position, revealing powerful double-jointed legs, but it stayed low to get out of the field of fire instead of attempting to pounce on the two deputies.

Stratton felt a sickening jolt of recognition when he saw the enemy's armor, though he couldn't quite place it in the heat of the moment.

The hesitation gave the enemy all the time it needed.

Marcone's gun went dry just as the armored figure, shrouded in the half-light of the subterranean environment, raised what appeared to be some manner of assault rifle and fired.

Deputy Marcone was picked up off his feet and launched across the small chamber slamming into the concrete wall. The high velocity rounds tore through the deputy's tactical armor like he was wearing simple cloth, Stratton knew they were out matched. Street gangs did not have this kind of armor or firepower, much less whatever abominations had emerged from the shadows to violently transform a simple tunnel purge into a massacre.

Stratton switched to full-auto and strafed the enemy, for the most part firing blindingly as he sprinted towards the tunnel exit. He was positive he had done little to damage the enemy, even if he did hear the impact of several rounds against its armor. He didn't stop to reload, or dare look twice at the grisly corpses of the other four men in his purge team as he fled the scene.

He didn't pay much attention to where exactly he ran, and soon was hopelessly lost in the endless subterranean system. That did not stop him from pressing on. Some part of his mind still held onto the knowledge that once he found a maintenance hatch or staff ladder he'd be able to gradually work his way to the surface through trial and error. Stratton's breath grew labored, each time he inhaled a sharp pain would race from his waistline up, across his right side. Running had never been his strong suit, even if he always passed his routine physical fitness exams. A deputy had to be able to perform the basics of their duties with full kit, which for a man on the special tactics unit meant body armor, utility harness, and at least one detainment net. Stratton was as fit as the average tactics man, though generally once the shooting started there was little reason for such sustained exertion.

He cursed at himself under his breath as he realized his rebreather was venting only on the left side. No wonder he was having trouble breathing down here, it was like having one lung doing the work of two. It didn't help that upon closer inspection, the armored enemy had grazed his side twice with nearly fatal shots.

Stratton knew he didn't have much time. Being unable to take a full breath, he accepted that there was little chance of survival anyway. Five men dead in less than two minutes, and the killers were something he even now could barely comprehend. Surely, he had not seen what he thought he had. Men who were not men, with limbs and eyes too alien to be anything but abomination.

There were lots of strange chemicals down here, also the gangers usually went in for bizarre costumes as part of their militant swagger. In the heat of the moment he must have imagined most of it.

"Just a bunch of gangers on the salts, probably laced with drift," he argued with himself as he struggled to breathe, knowing he was lying, but determined to buy a few more seconds of sanity before the walls came crashing down upon him. "Just people."

The deputy came to a halt in the middle of the cramped sewer tunnel and soon the shin deep water he'd been splashing through settled. He leaned against the wall for support and began fumbling for one of the replacement filters in his utility harness. His sub-machine gun hung on his chest, the strap rigged to allow him to go hands free when detaining a suspect or one of any number of things he might need both hands for. The stubby barrel was still hot from the last firefight and an acrid odor rose from it as the heat cooked off the water that had splashed it.

Even through the rebreather this place stank beyond belief, and for a deputy who had served for years in this dark underworld, that was a very bad sign indeed.

The great mega-city of Tankrid, named after the planet upon which it was the capitol, was a veritable ant hill of steel, glass, and concrete. With so many billions of human beings packed into such a dense urban environment, it took a vast sewer network to manage the sheer tonnage of waste. It was a seemingly endless honeycomb of tunnels, chambers, locks, and dams down here. Lots of places to conduct activities away from the ever-watchful eyes of the Marshal Corps.

Humanity was on the precipice of annihilation by the tooth and claw of the Extinction Fleet and yet, here he was, a sewer cop who wrangled human scum when the street gangs got too powerful. Tunnel purges were just part of the job, something that happened every six months or so, when one gang or another forgot its place. The elites of Tankrid didn't care at all what the human scum did to each other in the lower levels of the giant city, but when the crime waves splashed across their glittering lives there was hell to pay.

For all the courage and sacrifice of the Einherjar on those distant battlefields, human civilization had done little with the precious gift of time that the blood of heroes had bought over and over. We carry on much like we did before, thought Stratton as he swapped out the filters as quickly as he was able so that his hands could return to the comfort of his weapon. After three or four years, it seemed as if people barely remembered the old bad days before the Einherjar, where system after system fell before the enemy.

Stratton had never seen an Einherjar in person, but it felt, in moments like this, on these brutal tunnel purges, that the fearsome warriors of the All-Father were just the myths and the legends they were based on.

To patrol these grimy streets, to struggle with poverty and gang violence while elites sipped expensive tea and fresh food in their towers far above, one felt rather removed from such things.

His mind snapped to attention when he heard the unmistakable sound of something sloshing through the shallow water at the base of the tunnel. The sound of it made him think of the men who were not men that had torn his team to pieces. They were real, there was no denying it.

Stratton flexed his fingers around his weapon and continued towards the ladder, only this time faster as the scraping began to escalate in volume and urgency. Soon he could hear the pounding of feet against the concrete mixed in with the scraping and he wondered if the armored enemy was in pursuit as well.

He felt it more than he saw it when the first one appeared behind him. The deputy fired behind him as he kept scampering towards the ladder, fighting every instinct he had to go full-auto and instead laying down a steady beat of short bursts.

It was hideous to watch the thing that was not a man continue to charge him through his withering fire, as if the beast could not comprehend that it was marching to its own death.

Suddenly, he understood the tactic it was using, perfect for the confined environment with an enemy, him, who had finite amounts of ammunition. As the magazine clicked empty and the first beast fell, a fresh one leapt into the light to take its place.

Stratton roared then, filled with fear and anger in equal measure, and he dropped his sub-machine gun so that he could yank his pistol from its hip holster. He was an excellent marksman, something to make up for his achingly average fitness levels, and with great precision he put hollow point rounds through both of the monster's kneecaps. The deputy realized now that it took a full magazine, sometimes more, to bring down a single abomination, so he focused on buying himself some time.

The deputy had the last several minutes recorded with his body cam, and as the beast stumbled into the glow being cast by the service light at the top of the staff ladder, he was able to capture a clean view of it. Upon seeing it fully illuminated, Stratton turned and ripped off his rebreather just in time to vomit into the shallow sluice of fetid sewage. His mind struggled to make sense of the face that was not a face, the man who was not a man, and it was all he could do to place his hands on the ladder and begin to climb.

The beast thrashed with wounded fury, its voice straining against the limitations of the flesh it hid within.

A clawed hand grasped the bottom of the ladder.

Stratton pushed himself with every last ounce of will he had, ascending several rungs before he pointed his pistol down. The creature was slowly making its way up the ladder, limbs awkward and ill-suited for a conventional ascent despite the humanoid digits that hung limply from its form.

He emptied his magazine into the creature's head and chest, taking his time to line up his shots, slowly purging the creature from his mind as much as driving it away from his physical self. Finally, the creature let go of the ladder and splashed back down to the floor.

Stratton returned to climbing, realizing that the ladder led to a hatch that read "Hub LvL 2". If he could get that hatch open he'd be in the maintenance level, just underneath the busy streets of Tankrid. He was nearly there, if he could get the camera to command then his men would be avenged.

The deputy was bathed in yellow light as he reached the hatch. He reached up, his pistol discarded, and grasped the wheel that would turn and open the hatch.

There was a sudden stinging sensation in his lower back, and a wet sort of pressure that seemed to spread across his hips and groin. The deputy looked down and saw a ragged hole torn through his body armor, recognizing it for what it was, an exit wound.

It would take an armor-piercing round to punch through the plating on his back and then through his mid-section. He felt oddly detached from his own body. Somewhere in his mind he realized that this was his body's way of coping with the shock and trauma. The deputy found himself falling backwards, barely aware of his own weight as he sailed downwards.

He crashed into the ground at the base of the ladder, the height of the fall driving his armored form through the water and against the concrete to make a mighty splash. His helmet protected his skull with modest effect, and though he was positive he'd suffered a concussion, at least he was conscious. A fact that he soon regretted as he looked up to see the armored enemy standing above him, bathed in the sick yellow light from the hatch.

The deputy could not speak, the pain and shock was too much for him, so he said nothing when the armored enemy leaned over him and stretched out a metallic, clawed hand and snatched the body cam from his chest.

Stratton stared into the bright red glow of the enemy's armored helmet. He could see clearly now that it was, in fact, high end combat armor, though the shape of the thing wearing it was all wrong, too many joints and limbs far too long to be anything but abomination.

The armored enemy crushed the camera in its hand and let the broken pieces splash into the water next to the deputy. He wanted to scream at it, to challenge it, and yet, Stratton found he did not have the strength even for that. He was struggled mightily to stay conscious.

As the armored creature receded into the dark, one of the things that was not a man stepped into the light. This time, he could not look away, and for what seemed like an eternity he stared into those matte black eyes. He could sense the hunger in it, but there was pride there, too, ambition, and intellect. He felt true terror then, and as several more gathered around him, Stratton decided to stop fighting.

He closed his eyes and let go.

Better to sink into oblivion than to witness what was coming.

TRICKSTER CREATES THE WORLD

It was dark when he opened his eyes, and it was only by the soft whisper of a gentle breeze upon his dry pupils that the skald knew himself to be alive at all.

Upon achieving the awareness of his eyes, the veteran warrior began to concentrate on his breath, the first thing he had been taught when he was welcomed into the ranks of the Einherjar special forces. He focused on filling his lungs with air and expelling it slowly and with measured care. Soon he could feel the rising energy in his body, and he methodically tightened and relaxed his muscle groups one at a time.

It was not long until the skald's body crackled with kinetic potential, his fighting form warmed and limber, ready for anything. The entire process had taken less than a minute, but for him, it was nearly twice the time. He could not place himself in context to this lightless place, nor could he clearly imagine who he was in specific. That he was a warrior he recalled, a mighty operator in the service of the All-Father's army.

The skald attempted to rise from what he realized was a prone position, and became aware that he was naked and bound tightly. His chiseled form was pressed against a cold stone surface only marginally warmed by his flesh. He swallowed down the panic that suddenly threatened to overwhelm him, and intentionally lowered his heart rate as he rapidly regained control of himself. The skald strained against the bonds, less to break them and more to investigate them, taking note of the tightness and tensile quality of the bindings.

It was rope, but not the synthetic webbing material used by the Einherjar, more a crude length of woven fibers. It was the kind of rope that had not seen use in centuries, perhaps longer on the central planets. The machines that created such ropes no longer existed, and the craftsmen who wove them by hand were gone by a millennium.

As he moved carefully against the bindings the familiar scent of a woman enticed his senses.

Light from a torch soon illuminated what he saw was a small cave, and a beautiful woman came around a rough stone corner holding the torch aloft. Her long hair was tied behind her head to reveal a deep neckline, and as the flickering light danced across the ragged walls, her full lips seemed to glow. Upon seeing her, the skald's mind was flooded with memories of her, even if the fur mantle and simple spun dress she wore gave the impression of a costume rather than the modern clothing he recalled.

Ariana was her name, and she had been his wife.

His own name was lost in the darkness, yet the knowledge of her was sharp in his mind. Those memories stabbed at his heart, and he began to wonder with grim suspicion that this was some manner of hallucination or dream. Ariana had died during the grueling first years of the invasion, like the lost loves of a great many Einherjar, her body ground into so much raw organic matter upon the battlefields of Tarsis Prime.

The garm consumed all organic material available to them to keep the swarm active and effective. Every garm organism the Einherjar faced, after so many years of war, was no doubt in part comprised of the flesh of humanity just as much as it was the flora and fauna of any conquered plant. He wept as he watched her walk barefoot down a small and well-worn path from the mouth of the cave to the stone slab he'd been tied upon.

This was a resurrection dream, of that he no longer had any doubt, though in his long tour of duty he had not experienced anything so vivid. He watched as she set her torch into an iron ring bolted into the stone wall. She then knelt to pick something up. When she stood, the skald could see that she held a rough wooden bowl in her delicate hands.

She approached him and the warrior felt a knot begin to form in his chest, so badly did he wish to reach out and touch her. He dared not speak, at once for fear of giving her cause not to approach him and out of a disciplined approach to his captivity. While the garm were no takers of prisoners, each skald was immaculately trained to observe the conditions of a situation before taking reckless action.

As if in response to his silent wishes, Ariana came to stand next to the slab upon which the skald was bound. She set the bowl upon his chest and leaned in close, her hands running across his thickly muscled arms and her hair brushing against his forehead. She pressed her full lips to his and kissed him deeply as tears fell from her eyes and splashed against his cheek. Her touch was electric, and Skald Thatcher remembered himself.

He remembered Grendel.

The familiar bone-on-bone sound of the alpha garm filled the cave, and Ariana looked up from Thatcher. He did his best to follow her gaze despite his bondage and caught a glimpse of the mighty creature's reticulated body moving through the shifting shadows cast by the torch's light. Thatcher strained against the bonds and found himself held even tighter.

Ariana squeezed his shoulder as Thatcher watched Grendel slither into the light, its terrorizing visage just as nightmarish as he remembered. This beast had given him the hardest fight of his long life, and Thatcher had been found wanting. Despite wounding it numerable times the skald had fallen to its projectiles and barbed tail. His last sight of the beast had been of it lowering the wicked proboscis towards his face.

Thatcher's blood ran cold as he thought of the other men who had been slain by Grendel and had their minds plundered by the creature's unique bio-weapon. The resurrection would not hold, and there was a growing pile of torcs that contained the lives of men who could not be reborn. They always died again shortly after resurrection, most of them screaming and clawing at their own faces.

Grendel towered over Thatcher and Ariana, its teeth glistening and its chest shuddering as it extended its proboscis. The skald watched, helpless, as Ariana bravely stood in front of Grendel and picked up the bowl. A drop of bright green liquid dripped down from the garm's appendage, and as soon as it landed on Thatcher's face it began to burn and sizzle against his flesh. The skald did not flinch, unwilling to grant the alien beast the satisfaction, though the pain was very nearly unbearable.

A second droplet fell and this time Ariana positioned the bowl over Thatcher's face to catch it. Thatcher looked at his wife, a woman dead these many years, and began to understand what he was experiencing. More drops fell into the bowl and soon the only sounds to be heard in the cave were the crackling of the fire and the splash of the corrosive effusion. She wept as she held the bowl, already her arms trembling from the effort of holding it aloft even as it grew heavier with every drop.

Skald Thatcher was a believer in the 'narrative strategy' movement that had been growing in popularity amongst the various command elements of the Einherjar. That belief is what had encouraged him to request that his skald force be allowed to insert themselves into the Heorot campaign. There were too many serendipitous factors in this great struggle against the garm for a man like Thatcher to ignore, and when the garm attacked a settlement with the very name from myth, he'd known there was more at work in this struggle than a simple contest of beasts and bullets.

He had been arrogant, Thatcher told himself as Ariana struggled to keep the rapidly filling bowl steady, and convinced himself that he was the Beowulf of this tale. It seemed to make sense at the time, as he and his skalds joined the fighting only after the marine companies were taking a beating and barely able to hold the line. Like the ancient hero,

Thatcher and his warriors had laid a trap for the beast, and when battle was joined, the skald commander had met Grendel one on one. Their struggle had been mighty indeed, and yet, it was the monster who slew the thane as it were, and here the skald found himself.

The bowl was full, and as more drops fell the liquid threatened to slosh over the side. Ariana's lips trembled as much as her arms, and she looked down at Thatcher apologetically. She took a deep breath and moved the bowl. As she did, a drop landed on Thatcher's cheek, and he growled low as he fought against the near blinding pain.

The young woman turned and walked quickly across the cave to a hole in the floor where she dumped out the contents of the bowl.

Without the bowl to protect him, another drop fell from Grendel, this time on his nose, and then another on his lip. The skald fought the scream valiantly, every scrap of his willpower invested in remaining stoic in the face of this torture, and yet as more drops fell into his eyes he could not contain it any longer.

Skald Thatcher roared in pain and frustration, only to swallow more of the burning green fluid, which assaulted his vocal chords with caustic savagery. Ariana returned and positioned the bowl above his face, and after a few moments Thatcher calmed himself enough to focus on his breathing. The pain had been excruciating, and by the time he was able to recover he could see Ariana already beginning to struggle again with the bowl.

It was not long before she had to dump the bowl again, and once more Thatcher suffered in agony as Ariana rushed to return to him. The skald lost count of how many times it happened, and soon his world was reduced to moments of emptiness and fullness as his life was measured by the bowl. Such was the relentlessness of the mind shattering pain that for all the skald knew he could have been resurrected and died a thousand times, always returning to this single nightmare.

There was another story at work here, thought Thatcher madly, after what could have been years or mere minutes of torture underneath Grendel's dripping bio-weapon.

He watched Ariana hold the bowl over his face and thought of the Norse god, Loki. He was the trickster, the lord of misrule, and a bastard half-giant son of the god's own enemies. Thatcher recalled that Loki caused a great evil against the gods, and his punishment was to be bound to a stone and tortured. In the story, a serpent dripped poison onto Loki's face, his only respite being his wife Sigyn holding a bowl to protect him when she could. Until the end of days this would go on, a time when the world would be destroyed by titanic war and reborn from the ashes.

In between the seemingly endless bouts of blinding pain, Thatcher's mind began to fixate on the story. It was a lifeline that kept him from drowning in the caustic waters of torture. He clung to it with a fierce tenacity borne of a lifetime of war and loss, and eventually the skald found that he could handle the pain more than he could at the beginning. He was not immune by any stretch, though he found himself snarling with defiance each time Ariana was forced to move the bowl. He would endure.

Thatcher decided he had been wrong about his role in this great saga. There seemed little difference to him any longer between reality and the resurrection dream, and he determined that he would embrace the reality presented to him. Humanity had named the garm, and so warriors like him had risen to be the Einherjar. A distant settlement had been named Heorot, and so came Grendel.

His mind was consumed with the thought of Ragnarok, the Norse end of days, a glorious end to this grinding stalemate between humanity and the extinction fleet. A final contest between the Einherjar and the Garm.

Yes, he had been wrong, and he was never meant to be Beowulf.

Upon this acceptance, the skald's eyes opened and he found himself in the body forge, attended by Idris and surrounded by a dozen of his most loyal operators. To resurrect those slain by Grendel had been forbidden, and yet they had persisted despite protocol. No doubt trying over and over, undeterred by every repeated death, ever measured by the emptiness and fullness of the bowl. The man who used to be Skald Thatcher looked into the eyes of the assembled warriors and knew what had to be done.

He was fated to be Loki.

ANGRBODA

The Einherjar gunship slid through the void like a shark through the sea. The armored ceramic panels that covered it from bow to stern were made with a blend of volcanic ash that turned the ship into a matte black form set against the darkness of open space.

Compared to the larger Einherjar warships like the *Bright Lance*, or even the security frigates of the United Humanity Coalition, the gunships were small, though with fire power enough to accord themselves well in battle against the living ships of the extinction fleet.

Armed with four rotating chainfire weapons, each the size of what one would expect on a battle tank, and a small assortment of ship-to-ship rockets, the gunships were deadly craft when on the attack. They were rare vessels indeed, built exclusively in the shipyards of Prax and every one of them assigned to skald forces.

They were used predominantly as stealth vessels that could bite back if threatened, executing recon patrols, search and destroy missions, and high value troop insertions for the Einherjar special operators. A crew of engineers, pilots, gunners, and officers, twenty men in all, kept the ship flying, and it had the capacity to transport and deploy upwards of thirty warriors in full kit. By all accounts they were coveted pieces of equipment, and as a result several men had to die in order for Loki and his followers to make good their escape from the Bifrost.

Loki shook gently in his seat, the straps holding him in place as the gunship, now renamed *Angrboda* by the men who had seized it, tumbled in a tight roll to avoid the floating organic wreckage of what had once been a garm warship. From his vantage point behind the pilot's pulpit the warrior could see that the vast expanse of space was filled with dead and dying garm vessels. Behind them by many tens of thousands of miles, just out of scanner range, lay the great circular star fortress known as Bifrost, and in front of that even more carnage hung in the cold void.

Upon awakening, his followers had told him of the titanic assault launched by the extinction fleet, though it was not until he consumed the remains of Grendel that he understood the true intentions behind the attack. The memory of that heinous act was bright in his consciousness, and he found himself reaching up to rub his fingers across the inflamed resurrection injection sites at the base of his skull. It had been the hardest thing he'd ever done, taking that nightmare creature into himself.

It was the first step of a long and bitter journey, Loki thought to himself as he recalled the sickeningly sweet taste of Grendel's alien brain as he scooped it from the skull with his bare hand and ate it raw.

The psychic garm cells that rested inert in the beast's brain entered his system and awakened with the ferocity of lighting in a storm cloud, pairing with the cells that had been encoded into Loki's body by Grendel's proboscis fluids when they fought in the streets of Heorot, and he had now become something not quite human.

Loki looked at the pilot and took note of how the man's hand did not shake as he expertly brought the ship out of the roll and righted their course. The man had previously only been the co-pilot, a man in reserve, though both the chief pilot and the former ship's master had been unwilling to yield control of the ship to Loki's followers. The two men, along with two engineers, were now drifting in the frozen darkness of space thousands of miles behind them.

The already mythic status and reputation of the skald special forces, combined with the swift brutality of their seizure of the ship had brought the rest of the crew in line.

The traitor marine looked down at the five torcs that had been fastened to a bandolier and draped across his armored chest. Five men who had to die so that Loki could escape and go to meet his destiny. While those men would certainly be resurrected in the body forge, so long as he kept the torcs, they would have no knowledge of that particular life they'd lived. It was like this for all the men who served in the armies of the All-Father. It was not uncommon for a warrior to die and his torc to go unrecovered. Gaps in the memory of their lives was part of the sacrifice they made to fight as equals against the garm.

"Skald Thatcher, ahem, sorry. Loki, we are starting to get ping-backs on long range scans," announced the pilot, "I'm showing massive heat spikes and audible shockwaves. There's a hell of a fight going on out there, sir."

"I have felt it for some time now. Tune your instruments to the center of the storm, pilot, and take us in," responded Loki. He grit his teeth from the effort of resisting the psychic pressure of the Alpha Hive Mind. "I will direct you onwards once we have visual contact."

Upon awakening, he had been swiftly briefed by Idris and the other skalds. The man who used to be Skald Thatcher learned that he had been resurrected and died horribly dozens of times since first being killed by Grendel. He was told of the unassuming rifleman, Ajax, who continued to beat the odds, not only breaking away the beast's proboscis, but eventually slaying the beast in close quarters combat.

The man listened raptly as he was told of the heroic final stand of Jarl Mahora beneath the trophy of Grendel's severed head, and of how Ajax was the last man to fall, the corpses of the enemy at his feet. Beowulf had indeed emerged from within the ranks of Hydra Company.

As the *Angrboda* crept through the shattered corpses of garm bio-vessels, Loki fought off the continued psychic pressure of the Alpha Hive Mind.

While the man that people had taken to calling the Bloodhound might not realize it, there were two hive minds now, and upon inviting the essence of Grendel into himself, Loki made contact. Both Hive Minds wanted to dominate him, but he was a skald of many hardened years, and neither could fully take him. He understood from his communion with the Usurper, his own name for the Beta Hive Mind that has risen in his consciousness, the true mother of Grendel, that the titanic assault by the extinction fleet had been two-fold in its purpose.

The first was, of course, to smash through the Einherjar lines, destroy or bypass the Bifrost, and consume humanity. However, a more sinister purpose was to occupy the forces of humanity so overwhelmingly that a bloody garm civil war would go unnoticed. The Usurper was strong, but its own power was dwarfed by the might of the extinction fleet. What the *Angrboda* now flew through was the aftermath of that brief and savage insurrection.

The pressure of the Alpha Hive Mind increased, and Loki felt the desperation of the Usurper, pleading with him, for all its brood, to save it. It was a cunning and ambitious thing, this Usurper, not at all the brutal hunger made manifest that was the Alpha Hive Mind. The Usurper was just as much a dire enemy of the Hive Mind as the Einherjar were. Our purposes are aligned, thought Loki, as he keyed deployment prep commands to his team of operators.

Skald Unferth's icon glowed green on Loki's wrist display, indicating that the man had received the orders. Loki considered his men for a moment, and a surge of pride welled up inside of him, soon to be joined by a hollow dread at what must be done.

Idris belonged in the forge, and is was easy for him to cover his tracks, to obscure the fact that Skald Thatcher had been resurrected over and over, well beyond the threshold of protocols. Even the Watchman, esteemed as he was, had only been brought back twice before command deemed the way shut for all men whose minds had been plundered by Grendel. Thatcher's torc remained in the pile along with the other victims of Grendel, and none were the wiser that he lived again.

It was not so easy for Unferth and the other eleven skalds who now rode with Loki into hostile garm territory. The moment they murdered the security guard who watched over Grendel's severed head, they became blooded traitors to a man. The bonds of the skald ran deep, especially so with Thatcher's crew, one of the most decorated forces in the All-Father's great army. It was they who had been instrumental in throwing back the swarms on Orion 12, they who had led the Tardis sector purges, and each man among them had multiple WarGarm kills to his name. It was a testament to their loyalty and to the firmness with which they believed in the unfolding narrative strategy that they accepted him as Loki. Only in a universe where alien swarms threatened humanity with extinction could such hardened men choose to give themselves over to a half-remembered collection of myths from ancient Earth.

Much like the Norse warrior traditions upon which the Einherjar military had been founded, a marine's service record meant more than his life, doubly so for soldiers to whom death was just another journey. The old Vikings had called it 'wordfame', the idea that a man's deeds lived on in story and so his life mattered as long as his story was told. While the service record of the man named Thatcher remained untarnished, each skald who now prepared to die against the garm was marked a traitor. Their service records would bear that shame long after they were dead on whatever distant field their fate demanded. While they still wore their torcs, no body forge waited to honor their deaths with rebirth.

Now that the crew of the renamed *Angrboda* were sailing with them, those men would share the same eventual end. Loki needed himself and every skald aboard to execute the coming assault, which meant he had to leave the vessel in the hands of a crew he'd pressed into service at gunpoint. He knew it was a gamble to leave them without a skald to hold them fast, but there was no other way. Thirteen of humanity's most fearsome warriors would still only have a thin margin for victory as it was, much less being down a man just to keep the crew from mutiny. The time had come to see what this crew as made of, and how far he could stretch their sense of duty before they rose up against him.

The debris field of organic wreckage cleared and Loki was given a clear visual of the scene before him. A lone hive ship limped through open space, bearing the wounds of a savage space battle. Swarming over it were dozens of assault craft, each one having the appearance of a giant needle with a bulging sack attached to the base. Those aboard the *Angrboda* had seen this before, and recognized the craft as troop transports, each sack containing swarms of boarders. Usually the garm boarding parties consisted of clutches of gorehounds and ripper drones, with at least one Wargarm in command. The Ultragarm and ridgebacks were too large for effective shipboard action, and shriekers were barely combat effective once grounded, though that was little comfort when facing the alien menace in the tight confines of a spacecraft.

Drifting just off to the side of the hive ship was the gigantic corpse of a brood ship, which appeared to have launched all of its assault craft before being slain by the hive ship's weapons. Dozens of barbed projectiles impaled the brood ship. As it continued to tumble through the void, a garm spine frigate swept out from underneath it to attack the hive ship. It had apparently been using the dying brood vessel as cover, and soon was exchanging a catastrophic amount of firepower with the already wounded hive ship. Upon closer inspection, the tentacle appendages of the hive ship were even now crushing another frigate. With no garm ships loyal to the Alpha Hive Mind anywhere within scanner range or close enough to apply additional psychic pressure on Loki's mind, he knew that the power of both garm fleets was all but spent, and that these were the last moments of a battle long won by the Alpha Hive Mind.

"Pilot, you will notice the third assault craft embedded on the aft section of the ship, that's our insertion point. Set the drop launcher to punch us through just above it, where the hull is already weak," ordered

Loki. "Gunners, keep a weather eye for that spine frigate. While it is likely to focus upon the other garm vessel, we will need to destroy it in order to accomplish the extraction and make our escape."

"The extraction, sir?" asked the gunnery chief, as he turned in his chair to face Loki.

The warrior looked at the gunnery chief and they held each other's gaze for a moment, before the chief backed down and returned to his duties. Loki took a deep breath as the ship neared weapons range, then keyed the command channel to speak. It was now or never.

"Men of the *Angrboda*, you have suffered much indignity. Your comrades have been put to death and your ship seized, and yet you serve at your post with skill and poise. In the battle ahead there may be opportunities for you to mutiny, and to do so is your right.

The skalds who are about to fight and die today have made their choice. You were never given that chance. I say that you will have that choice soon. If honor demands it, rise up and do your worst," spoke Loki over the command channel, his deep voice filling the ears of every man aboard the gunship, from skald to crew. "Though take heed, we are about humanity's business this day, and foul as it may seem, every blow we strike is for our people, even those whose blood yet stains our hands. There is only darkness and winter ahead, we go onwards without hope for a spring or a respite from carnage, and that is the source of our strength. Fight with me, brothers, and let us show them what men can do."

There was no battle cry raised, no shouts for glory, only the grim silence of the task at hand. Loki unfastened his straps and left the bridge, swiftly descending the ladder to the troop hold as the ship shook with activity.

He hoped what he'd said was enough, because if it wasn't, then no matter how the mission on board the hive ship went he and his men would have no extraction and it would have been for naught. It was such a risk, such a brazen gambit, and yet he felt firm in his choice. The ship's crew were Einherjar just as much as the infantry divisions who died upon the claws in the dirt. They would do their duty.

Loki strapped himself into one of the drop pods that the launcher would hurl at the enemy ship. Now that his course was set, he could feel the Usurper's psychic pressure beginning to push back against that of the Alpha Hive Mind. It knew he was coming, and it fought to help him maintain control. The ship bucked and spun, and Loki could feel the staccato recoil of the chainfires reverberating through the ship. Over his crew channel he listened as the pilot threaded his way through the space battle. The gunnery chief lashed out at the spine frigate and the Alpha Hive Mind's assault craft that had not yet disgorged their full complement of boarders.

Loki felt the surge of power in their voices, and knew that his speech had worked. Now that battle was joined, the crew of the *Angrboda* had set aside their questions, their doubts burned away in the fire of a good hard fight.

"Drop launch in five minus," said the pilot as the warning lights in the pods began to flash yellow, "We will engage the spine frigate and wait for the extraction order. *Angrboda* out."

Loki let out a breath he had not realized he'd been holding. They took the name, which meant they took the mission.

"Good hunting," said Loki just as the pods rocketed out of their housing and hit vacuum.

LORD OF MISRULE

The door of the drop pod burst outwards, and in the space of a breath, the skalds emerged with guns blazing. Loki leapt out of the pod and instantly found himself in a target rich environment. The assault craft they landed above had not yet disgorged its full complement of boarders, and through the massive tears in the flesh of the living ship, Loki could see them pouring out of the aperture of the craft's hollow needle prow.

They had deployed right into the thick of the enemy attack force, but there had been no other way. The drop pods were stout, but not designed for penetrating the thick hide of the garm vessels. They could handle the heat of orbital insertion, but were not designed for use against the garm.

It was just another example, in Loki's thinking, of how the oppressive presence of the Hive Mind had pushed humanity into a siege mentality. We have never developed ways to attack the garm, only to defend against them, and that's how the extinction fleet wants it, thought Loki as he cut a ripper drone in half with a burst of fire, so we must adapt with such reckless tactics as this.

The skalds were consummate fighters, in the deadly close quarters conflict with the garm, their superior training and weapons discipline gave them a distinct edge. In seconds, the garm boarding party's attack was blunted as the skalds cut a swathe through them to establish a kill zone for themselves. Scores of garm perished in the furious brawl, the aliens unprepared for the sheer brutality of the skald's entry onto the battlefield. Two skalds were already lying in pieces upon the fleshy deck of the ship, but bought with their lives was a solid fighting position for the others.

As Unferth and the others laid down suppressing fire with their pulse rifles in order to maintain the perimeter, gunning down enemies as they attempted to exit the garm assault craft, Loki took a knee and reached out with his mind.

The Usurper was aware of his presence upon its hive ship, and Loki could feel it howling in pain as boarders ravaged it from stern to bow. Open yourself to me, said Loki with his mind, casting his consciousness ahead of him like he imagined a bat might do with sonar in the perfect darkness of a terrestrial cave. In an instant he felt a pull, deeper into the ship, and though he could not consciously tell where he *should* go, he was certain that his feet would take him where he *needed* to go.

"Skalds, on me!" shouted Loki as he sprang to his feet and pushed through a large tear in the fleshy interior wall of the ship.

They had punched through the hull, but unlike human ships, the membranes of the living garm vessels prevented rapid decompression, one of the unique advantages they had evolved in order to cope with space travel. The garm adapt, Loki thought grimly as he raised his pulse rifle and shot a ripper drone in the face. Two more came rampaging down what Loki could only describe as some kind of ribbed hallway, and he brought them into his iron sights.

Unferth was suddenly at his side, and the two men reduced the drones to so much smoking meat in the blink of an eye. Roars of angry hunger erupted behind them, and they turned to see the hallway beginning to fill up with drones.

At first, Unferth moved to fire upon them, but Loki put his hand on the man's pulse rifle to prevent him from firing. Loki nodded in the direction of the drones and Unferth saw that the drones had stopped their advance, poised to attack, and yet holding their position as they looked at the Einherjar with their glossy black eyes. Something was holding them back, and Loki felt that it must be the Usurper.

Suddenly, the rippers of the Alpha Hive Mind lived up to their name by using their scything blades to cut their way through the walls, making room for gorehounds to move through the gaps and bring their projectile weapons to bear. The two garm forces began to tear into each other with a frenzied bloodlust that Loki had not encountered in all his years fighting the garm. This must have been what the likes of Ajax and Hydra Company had witnessed on the barren wastes of Heorot when the swarms murdered Grendel's hive ship.

Loki turned away from the sickening carnage and rushed down the opposite hallway, letting his instincts guide him. Soon the hallway opened up into a central hub that led to several apertures in the spongy interior. The hub was awash in gore as swarms of garm loyal to the Alpha Hive Mind were in the last moments of slaughtering a clutch of the Usurper's drones, leaving only a lone WarGarm desperately defending itself.

"*Fangs out!*" bellowed Loki as he raised his rifle and sent a bolt through the neck of an enemy gorehound.

The thirteen warriors strode forward in a v-shaped formation, with Loki functioning as the tip of the spear, each of them laying down punishing fire with the sort of discipline that took years to perfect. Loki fired his ten rounds with devastating effect and then with fluid efficiency used one hand to guide the rifle along its sling to his back racking the slide to vent the rifle's accumulated heat. With his other hand he pulled his pistol from its holster and raised it to fire with a speed that others would have to work years to master.

Loki was not the only one to conduct such a maneuver, the tactic being a standard part of skald training for such blitz attacks. The skald sidearms were designed for this tactic, and their carbon mags only held ten rounds. As he emptied his magazine he depressed the ejector, and the hollowed-out magazine rocketed to the ground, propelled by the venting heat of the weapon. Without breaking stride, Loki slammed his pistol over one of the magazines mounted on his thigh plate and then slid the pistol back into his holster while with his other hand slinging the now vented rifle back into forward position.

His pulse rifle roared again, and yet more garm organisms screamed and died. By the time Loki and the other skalds needed to vent again, they had reached the center of the chamber. As the other skalds repeated the pistol swap and continued to punish the remaining hostiles, Loki entered melee range with the WarGarm.

The mighty beast leveled its weapons at Loki as the skald slung his rifle and neglected to draw his pistol. Loki sharpened his mind and sent his consciousness slicing through the space between them. In an instant, he felt the psychic pressure of the WarGarm as its instinct pushed it to attempt to control his mind and his actions, since he seemed to register in its simple mind as part of its own swarm. The beast was confused at the complexity of Loki's mind, and it bared its teeth menacingly as he stood before it. The monster's face was but a few inches from his own when Loki roared with voice and with mind.

His consciousness bowled over the intellect and will of the WarGarm, and it stopped its advance. The beast was held in thrall as Loki pushed himself deeper into its being. Inside the psychic fog that was the WarGarm's alien mind, Loki found its connection to the Usurper, envisioning it as a tiny silver thread leading into the distant unknown behind the fog. The WarGarm slowly lowered its weapons and backed away, its head down in a clear signal of submission.

Unferth and the other skalds were venting heat and reloading fresh carbon magazines as they stood in a protective formation around Loki.

The WarGarm turned slowly and began walking towards one of the dozen apertures in the central hub. Loki followed the beast, and Unferth, knowing what his master was attempting, gestured to the rest of the men to flank the pair on either side.

Loki felt the WarGarm sending psychic commands to the other defenders of the ship. The skald knew that the organisms that had been fighting desperately to protect the ship were now leaving it to die. All focus had shifted to one section of the ship, and it was there that Loki knew his destiny would finally take shape.

"I have made contact and the hive is with us. The ship's defenders are moving to run interference for our advance," said Loki over the squad channel. "You have been briefed on the subtle differences between friendlies and hostiles, but follow your own judgement when the time to fight is upon us."

It was not long after making his statement that their formation was attacked on two sides by swarms of the enemy, though as he suspected, the beleaguered defenders of the ship began to appear.

Loki soon lost track of where he was in the ship as they fought a running battle through the labyrinthian corridors and cyclopean chambers of the hive ship. The Alpha Hive Mind seemed to have sussed out what they were fighting to reach, as resistance continued to escalate most of the remaining defenders hurled themselves into the fray.

Loki allowed himself to run on instinct, sinking into a sort of battle trance as they moved through the ship. The Usurper's presence in his mind began to overshadow and drive out that of the Alpha Hive Mind, and Loki realized that if he'd been fighting to keep the Usurper out he'd have likely had a seizure. It was only their common purpose that kept his mind from being turned to ruin, and the veteran operator took note of that hard truth. He was in the Usurper's dominion now, and as aliens died in droves to escort him and the skalds through the ship, it was clear that without their help this mission would have ended much sooner.

The warrior slapped a fresh magazine into his pulse rifle and found himself entering a wide chamber filled with a nearly oppressive amount of heat and humidity. He had never been inside the central brood chamber of a hive ship, though he had read a multitude of intelligence briefings that constituted the sum of the Einherjar's knowledge of such things, which arguably was precious little.

Before him lay a wide pool filled with a glowing green fluid, and he could feel the Usurper's psychic presence emanating from it. The WarGarm was dying, having taken a number of grievous wounds during their violent march through the ship, and it sank to the floor just at the edge of the pool.

"Fagan, pull security," ordered Loki as he set his rifle against the edge of the pool and began unfastening his armor, "Unferth, attend me."

With the two of them focusing on the task, Loki was able to get his armor removed and strip away his body glove much faster than if he'd done it alone. The remaining six skalds fired into the sporadic groups of attackers that managed to fight their way into the central chamber. The sounds of horrific carnage just outside were near deafening, as every last garm defender had answered the call and was fighting with a desperate ferocity to buy the skalds life moment to moment.

Loki, now fully naked, climbed over the edge and lowered himself into the pool. The communications from the Usurper had been like a dream, and yet now that he was finally experiencing the pool, it was an altogether unexpected sensation. The alien mind had shown him what waited here, just beneath the viscous waves. Loki's feet touched the terraced ribs of the pool's floor, and he waded deeper into the liquid until finally, he disappeared beneath the gently swirling waves.

Unferth was a loyal skald and a believer in Loki's apocalyptic mission. A lifetime of war against the garm had opened his mind to much in the way of possibility. When the myths of ancient Earth began to manifest in his waking life, right before his eyes, the skald believed. Unferth had fought Grendel alongside the man who used to be Thatcher, and he'd been the one to carry his commander's torc to the body forge.

He had been a family man once, many lifetimes ago, and he had filled the hole in his heart with faith. Unferth needed for there to be more at work in the universe than jockeying for position on the food chain. Before serving under Skald Thatcher, he'd thought of the fact that his name, Unferth, appearing in the Beowulf saga as a simple coincidence, now he knew otherwise.

The surface of the pool was broken as Loki rose from the depths, and Unferth wept at the sight of it. The man's body was covered in tiny snail-like organisms that clung to his flesh, and in his powerful arms Loki cradled three writhing larval creatures. Loki's face had changed, and as the warrior watched muscles moved under skin and bone seemed to warp and change right before his eyes.

"*Angrboda*, prepare for extraction," said Unferth as he marveled at the sight before him, "Mission success."

The endless cycle of predator and prey be damned, they trod the path of destiny.

PAPER TARGETS

Ajax cast his sight across the vast sunlit oceans of Kai Prime, and found himself taken aback by the aquatic planet's beauty. The marine attempted to recall when last he'd seen such a vision of unspoiled nature, and was saddened that he could not.

Years of endless war had all but painted over his memories, and it seemed to him that the universe was a collection of ruined worlds, shattered by conflict. The bright blue of the waters, capped with frothy white as waves crested and broke against the rocky coastline, stirred within him something akin to melancholy, as he tried and failed to recall whether or not Rowan had loved the sea.

His wife had died in the early stages of the extinction fleet's invasion, though beyond the dim recollection of her beautiful face and the warmth of her smile, Ajax could not hold a memory of her firm in his mind. Only in the resurrection dreams, those fevered hallucinations that often assailed the Einherjar marines in that enigmatic state between life and death as the digital imprint of their minds was pressed into new cloned bodies, did she come into crisp focus.

A consciousness consumed by war eternal was the price of functional immortality, Ajax told himself firmly in an attempt to shake himself loose from thoughts that did not serve him, such was the cost of being a champion for humanity. Recycled heroes called to arms against wave after wave of ravenous alien swarms. There was a grim sort of poetry to that, and considering the mythic source of the entire Einherjar war effort, and the marine supposed it fitting.

There was more at work in his thoughts than the struggle to remember the more intimate details of his life, as the psychic pressure of the garm Hive Mind was ever-present for Ajax. The alien cells in his brain may have given him a significant advantage when it came to hunting down the more psychically active garm organisms, but it took a significant amount of energy and focus for the marine to keep it in check. He might have impressions of the enemy, but it, too, had some sense of him, and it was only through the intense meditation techniques taught to him by the skalds that he was able to manage the swirling chaos that had become his consciousness. It struck Ajax as rather interesting that when he looked into the watery expanse he found the pressure eased, the psychic burden lessened somehow.

Ajax was not the only marine taken with the sight of so much open water, and he noticed that Sharif stared into the deep blue with just as much intensity as he had a moment ago.

The other marine was strapped into a seat across from Ajax, the low-flying troop transport, with its open bay doors was a welcome change from the cramped APCs that were the standard deployment vehicle. Wind whipped sharply around them. Sharif saw Ajax looking at him and the marine activated his comms, his voice clear in the other marine's earpiece.

"Ajax, have you ever seen an ocean before?" asked Sharif as he turned his head back to look out at the open water, his pulse rifle cradled against his armored chest. "I think maybe I have, back when I was a kid, but the details are kind of fuzzy."

"I'm sure I have, the sound of the waves is really familiar, but nothing clear," shrugged Ajax as the internal warning lights began to strobe in a dull red, indicating that they were one minute away from the drop zone.

"That's how it goes," stated Yao from his seat next to Ajax as the transport began to speed up, "Fill our minds with guns and garm, there just isn't room for much else."

"You guys are bumming me out," interrupted Rama from his seat at the bay door on the other side of the transport as he gestured towards the glittering sea rushing beneath them. "This beats every miserable place we've visited since this whole thing started. Maybe we can't remember who we were before, and probably this too will go away eventually, but we're here now and its gorgeous. Shut up and enjoy it."

"Yeah, for another twenty seconds," Ford snorted from his seat as he ejected the carbon magazine from his pulse rifle and slapped it against his armored thigh before slotting it back into the rifle. "The skalds said the whole island is hostile ground, I think we're about to get all the wild nature we can handle."

"Hydra Company, we hit the drop zone in ten seconds!" boomed the voice of Jarl Mahora over the company channel, aboard one of the other transports that streaked across the sky. "Make 'em hurt, marines!"

Ajax flexed his armored fingers around the grip of his own pulse rifle and took a deep breath, held it for a moment, and then began to let it out slowly. It had been months since the nightmarish events on Heorot, and the marines were eager to get back into the fight. The *Bright Lance* and its legion of Einherjar warriors had been seconded to the newly formed 'Task Force Grendel' under the leadership of Skald Wallace and his special forces operators.

The mission of the task force was simple, to root out and eliminate any garm activity outside of the prime battlefront. The conflict on Heorot had been categorized as a garm weapons test, and though it had been thwarted by the marines, they all knew it was only the beginning of a new and gruesome phase in the war against the extinction fleet.

Ajax jostled in his seat as the transport banked hard to the right, and he considered the current deployment. The marines aboard the Bright Lance had been informed that during the final battle for Heorot, the garm had swarmed the prime battlefront in a titanic expenditure of strength. The Einherjar blockade had been penetrated in several places across the galaxy, and alien vessels entered human space. Those few vessels were relentlessly engaged and destroyed by both Einherjar warships and the conventional security frigates of the mere decade's old UHC government, the United Humanity Coalition.

The fighting at the blockade had been hideous, but the marines held firm despite heavy losses. The cost of all-out assault had been catastrophic for the alien invaders, and it was only the significant casualties inflicted upon the army of the All-Father that prevented an Einherjar counter-attack. The extinction fleet had broken itself upon the ramparts of humanity and across the multitude of systems that comprised the prime battlefront, the enemy lost its hold on vast swathes of territory as a result.

The coastline rushed up to meet the transport. Ajax felt the pilot throw on the reverse thrusters and knew battle would soon be joined. Ajax had worked with the skalds to help them determine where the newest monsters would rise, operating under the assumption, more like the crystal-clear certainty, that the enemy had more such experimental deployments in store.

At first the presence of the Hive Mind in the consciousness of Ajax had all but faded, as if the alien intellect itself had been spent in the vicious fighting, but as the days turned to weeks after the galaxy-wide battle, Ajax had begun to feel the psychic pressure again. Whatever rage the Hive Mind had spent upon the attack of the blockade had brought the marine's awareness of the enemy down to little more than a whisper, barely an impression of the alien intelligence's presence in his mind. However, the psychic burden began to grow once more, and away from the prime battle front, emanating from within human space.

At the insistence of a growing number of skalds, including Omar, part of the daily intelligence and strategy meetings were devoted to the study of old Norse myths and stories. It was at the intersection of one such story and a star chart of Kai Prime that the enemy was revealed.

The transport shuddered as its momentum was temporarily held in suspension by the reverse thrusters. The warning lights ceased strobing and went solid. As the transport halted, the co-pilot hit the release on the seat restraints, unleashing the marines to do their bloody work.

Ajax and Sharif leapt out of the transport and as their boots splashed down in the shallow water of the rocky beachhead, they had their rifles up and were peering down their iron sights. Ajax moved forward to make more room for the marines disembarking behind him.

The air in front of him was cloaked in roiling steam from the thrusters as they vaporized the salty coastal waters and remained hanging there thanks to the near oppressive levels of humidity.

It was a work of spontaneous brilliance on the part of Jarl Mahora that the marines deployed just off the coast, disembarking into waist deep water instead of the hard, dry ground further ahead. Two hundred and fifty marines stormed the beach under cover of a wall of steam, and as Ajax advanced he was thankful for it.

As the shriekers that defended this modest rocky island fired blindly into the encroaching mass of steam, salvos of corrosive liquid sputtered in the churning waters since the vast majority of them missed their targets.

A marine who strode beside Ajax shouted in pain as a one of the shriekers scored a lucky hit. The instant the caustic ordinance sprayed his ceramic combat armor, the man beneath it dissolved into a sickly greenish-red soup. The ruined corpse of the marine collapsed in the shallow surf and the only clue that he'd been charging through it only moments before was the clouding of the churning blue waters where he'd fallen.

It would have cost fewer resources and marine lives to simply punish the island with orbital bombardment and allow it to sink beneath the waves, but Ajax knew this needed to be a different sort of battle. They weren't here just to slaughter garm swarms, they were here for answers to a riddle they all hoped to unravel before the enemy could perfect its own answer.

The psychic presence of the garm surged within Ajax, and had he not spent months learning to control his relationship with it, he might have been overcome and splashed to knees. As it was, he controlled his breath and narrowed his awareness through the tiny groove in his iron sights. He might be able to track the more advanced garm breeds, like the Wargarm, or in theory, other prototype creatures like the horror named Grendel he'd killed on Heorot, but none of that would matter if he died on the beachhead. Now was the time to shoot and advance.

As Ajax emerged from the wall of steam his sights were filled with alien bodies. The island was only a few square miles large, and with the entire Hydra Company on the attack, they were coming at the objective from all sides.

Ajax squeezed the trigger of his pulse rifle and sent a super-heated bolt of plasma through the thorax of a shrieker. He could not help but smile wickedly as the beast exploded in midair, showering the ground with smoking viscera. It felt good to kill these wretched abominations, and suddenly it was the only thing that mattered to him.

Ajax was flanked by more rifles as the marine force crossed the last few meters of open ground before they reached the modest cover provided by the jagged boulder field. He continued to fire while a low growl built in his throat, his adrenaline surging as his aim tore through another of the garm fliers. When he reached the cover of the first boulder, crouching to avoid the corrosive return fire, Ajax focused again on his breathing.

These thoughts of mindless carnage did not serve him any better than the fruitless effort of delving into his obscured memories, and he knew he had to get control of himself. Losing oneself to the bloodlust was how a marine blacked out, and when that happened there was no coming back. Men were not created to exist in this endless cycle of violent death and swift resurrection, and those who could not maintain their psychological equilibrium were doomed to become berserkers.

The Einherjar war machine had been built to be a self-sustaining endeavor, with everything from their bullets to their very flesh being a somewhat renewable resource. Sadly, it had become more and more apparent over time that their minds were not so interchangeable as their bodies or their equipment.

Ajax shook his head as he let out another breath, and tucked the stock of his rifle into his shoulder once more.

"You good, brother?" asked Ford as he took cover near Ajax after snapping off several shots.

"Had to shake off the black," said Ajax as he stood, suddenly keenly aware of the loss of his friend Boone, the grenadier, who had succumbed to the psychological trauma during their bloody struggle with Grendel. "I'm online."

"Ripper drones in the boulder field!" came the voice of Mahora, and Ajax shared a nod with Ford before the two of them scrambled out from behind their boulders and moved forward.

The boulder field might provide them with a modicum of cover from the shriekers who roosted near and upon the stone pillar at the center of the island, but the close confines of the rugged terrain would favor the claws and scything blades of the rippers.

Ajax held his rifle in middle guard, ready to fire more by instinct than true aim in the close quarters fighting he expected to erupt any second now. As if on cue, a ripper drone emerged from behind a nearby pillar and charged the two marines. Bolts from both Ajax and Ford splattered the beast across the boulders, but no sooner had they slain that one, two more leapt into the fray.

Ford took a knee as he fired at the furthest of the two drones, the swift decision saving his life as the scything blade of the drone nearest swept through the empty air where his head was a second prior.

The ripper drones were simple creatures, with little in the way of critical thinking, and once they locked onto a prey target it was difficult to shift their attention away until the prey was eliminated. This reality made them devastating shock troopers, and many an Einherjar position had been overwhelmed by the sheer ferocity of the drone rush that was often the swarm's opening move in any conflict. However, in this case, a more advanced garm organism might have carried the momentum of their attack towards Ajax and given up on Ford, but the drone had locked onto the kneeling marine. The ripper pivoted on its double-jointed feet and brought its other claws and blades around in a wide arc in an attempt to impale its prey.

Ajax and Ford had fought the garm side by side many times over the years, and while the kneeling marine focused on killing the drone he fired upon, there was complete trust that Ajax would keep him covered. Ajax held steady and squeezed the trigger of his pulse rifle, the first bolt punching through the shoulder of the drone and spinning it back around to face him, while the second and third shattered the chitin plates covering its chest and protecting the vital systems within.

The drone staggered backwards, still perilously close to Ford, who was already firing upon a third drone that rushed the pair from the same direction. Ajax fired once more, this time his bolt pounded into the drone's exposed chest, the heat and pressure of the round causing the drone to explode from the inside out.

Sharif appeared on the marine's right flank, his rifle aimed upwards as he gunned down a shrieker. Yao, Silas, and Rama sped past the shooters and plunged deeper into the boulder field. Ford rose to his feet and joined Sharif and Ajax as they followed the other marines.

These five marines had become a circle of friends over the years, observed Ajax as he ran behind the group and watched them raise rifle to battle another wave of drones, though he could not recall exactly why they had gravitated towards each other. So little remained of the men they had once been, before the war, before the blessing and curse of the torcs they wore that captured their experiences and enabled them to resurrect in the body forge. What would make one marine feel that kinship with another, out of an entire legion of warriors, much less a group of them, if not some scrap of their former identity? Such loose knit groups of comrades were common throughout the Einherjar ranks, though none could say what forged their bond, for none among them could recall the sorts of details that formed the basis of friendship amongst civilians and conventional military men.

Ajax laughed to himself as he added his firepower to Rama's to bring down a ripper that attempted to sweep up on their left flank. To fight the garm they had to become similar to them, disposable combatants without the cluttered distraction of vibrant three-dimensional humanity. The marines had only the basest levels of personality, himself included, and yet in the furious press of combat it was those base traits that held these thinly defined men true to each other.

We've made ourselves like them in order to win, thought Ajax as he ejected his spent carbon magazine and slapped a fresh one in the slot with the sort of mechanical discipline that took years to achieve, but we're still men. We feel the heat of victory, the sting of defeat, and the pain of loss when the warriors who stand with us fall to tooth and claw.

Indeed, he had no idea what sports teams he preferred, what it had been like growing up on whatever planet he'd once called home, or that he could not recall the last words he'd exchanged with his long dead wife. Such things had been sacrificed for his keen understanding of garm anatomy, roared Ajax in his mind as he shattered the knee of a sprinting drone, causing it to stumble and giving Silas a clean shot at its head. In place of a clear picture of his parents Ajax had the knowledge required to field strip his armor and equipment for cleaning and repairs, along with seemingly infinite tactical responses to the oncoming enemy.

Lost were the memories of happier times and gained was the intimate understanding of how to press the fight even after sustaining grievous wounds that would have sent any other soldier into a state of shock.

Ajax saw Ford go down, the man's left leg sheared off just above the knee. Sharif blasted the ripper drone into smoking pieces a moment later.

A caustic stream splattered into the boulder just next to Ajax, and he was forced to rip off his shoulder pauldron as the vile fluids rapidly ate through much of the armored plating. As fast as he could Ajax raised his rifle and returned fire, and as the corpse of the shrieker plummeted to the ground the marine saw that much of the sky had been emptied of the creatures. He took aim on another that was strafing a distant part of the boulder field, and cursed as his bolts flew wide. The pulse rifles were devastating at mid to close range, yet lost much of their effectiveness at distance.

Ajax fired again, more out of frustration than anything, and missed once more. Just as he started to lower his rifle and turn it back upon opponents nearer to his position a loud cracking sound cut through the cacophony of battle, and the distant shrieker shuddered from the impact of a heavy round.

Ajax spun on his heels and returned his attention to the boulder strewn field ahead of him, freshly reminded that Hart, one of the Einherjar snipers and the sixth man in their modest band of brothers, was out there dealing death at a distance. The marine saw that the boulders were beginning to thin out, which made it a blessing that the shrieker swarm had been significantly thinned. His comrades had established a firing line and were being pressed hard by waves of ripper drones.

As Ajax rushed to join them, he saw Silas pause in his shooting and move to reload. In the brief reprieve from punishing fire, one of the ripper drones skirted across their line, using a low boulder to soak up a few bolts, and managed to reach the marine. Just as Ajax got his rifle up, the beast tore into Silas, its blades and claws rending the armored marine into several bloody pieces as the ripper made good on its name. Sharif turned and tried to bring his rifle around, but just as he did, another drone emerged from behind a taller boulder and leapt off of it, sailing through the air towards the distracted marine.

Ajax switched to full-auto and cut loose on the beast as it descended towards Sharif as the other marine annihilated the gore-covered ripper that had murdered Silas. Ajax held tightly onto his pulse rifle as it kicked hard against him, spitting round after round wildly as he kept it pointed at the leaping drone. The creature's body was heavy enough that even though it was torn asunder as it was struck multiple times by bolts from Ajax it managed to strike Sharif. The marine was knocked off his feet by the broken corpse of the drone, though Ajax was relatively sure he'd not been injured by it.

Another drone was cut down on the right flank and Ajax looked down to see that even though he was rapidly bleeding out from his shorn leg, Ford was still in the fight. A normal man might have passed out by now, from the blood loss if not the pain, but like Ajax, the marine had become something harder than a normal man, something forged upon the anvil of endless war. Ajax, hoping to buy Ford a few more minutes of combat effectiveness, knelt down next to the wounded marine.

"This is going to hurt," said Ajax as he slid his booted foot under Ford's leg to raise the wounded stump off the ground.

Ford said nothing, simply gritting his teeth and swapped out his empty magazine for a fresh one. Ajax held the breach of his weapon near the ragged wound, and then pulled back the slide. The pulse rifles built up tremendous amounts of heat as they were fired, and after every ten shots they needed to be vented in order to prevent an automatic shutdown. The ejected heat instantly cauterized Ford's wound, and while the man roared in pain, at least he would not bleed out anytime soon. If he survived the battle a new limb could be grown, and if he did not the torc would be used to resurrect him. As it was Ajax dosed his comrade with combat meds, giving the wounded man enough of a boost to hold his rifle steady as Ajax lifted him up using one arm.

The two men turned back to the marine firing line to see that Sharif was back on his feet and the group was ready to move out. There were still several dozen meters of boulder field to clear before they reached the base of the tower, and they needed every rifle they could get. Ajax nodded at Sharif and the marine gave the signal to press onwards.

From a tactical perspective, it was madness to attack a garm held position, given that in general the garm wanted the enemy closer, as the garm were far superior to the marines in close quarters fighting. Yet here they were, marching towards the enemy instead of holding a line against them, and to Ajax it felt good. Humanity was on the offensive, and the aliens were struggling to cope.

Ajax and Ford combined their fire to annihilate a drone that attempted to slip up behind the marines, the alien beast having likely moved in from attacking another group, judging by the gore still dripping from its maw.

Ford was quaking as he struggled to stand, and even with the help of Ajax it was clear that soon he would be done. Just ahead of them, Rama and Yao took another shrieker out of the sky, leaving the air above them finally empty of alien threats.

When Yao lowered his rifle to vent the heat, a great roar sounded across the battlefield and more of the drones hurled themselves recklessly against the firing line. Ajax watched as Yao fired from the hip on full-auto and splattered two drones before a third, heedless of having had several of its limbs blasted off, careened into the human warrior.

Rippers had been bred by the extinction fleet to be mindless combat drones, and were by design, not equipped with a survival instinct, much less fear. The beast drove one of its body blades through Yao's mid-section as it crushed the marine's helmet with its hideous, fanged jaws. The marine continued to fire as he went down and the alien and human died together. Only the automatic venting protection kept Yao's weapon from taking out any of his nearby comrades.

Ajax and Ford poured their own fire into the gap in the line left by Yao's death and another drone was pasted across the rocky ground. Ford's one leg finally gave out and the marine collapsed, falling away from Ajax as he dropped his rifle in exhaustion.

Ajax didn't have the chance to kneel and check on his comrade, as the furious last charge of the drones raged against the dwindling firepower of the marines. It was this relentless drone assault that had overwhelmed the marine trench networks just as many times as it had broken against the ramparts, only this time the Einherjar were on open ground.

Ajax kept shooting, maintaining his firing discipline with a keen understanding that the only way out of this situation was to kill absolutely everything on the island.

The drones, and most of the garm broods for that matter, only attacked, never retreated, and if they did withdraw, it was only to maneuver for a better angle. The drones continued to rush into the blazing guns of the marines until at last, the corpse of the final beast smacked wetly against the ground in front of the marines.

Sharif gave the hand signal to advance, and the handful of marines in the assault squad who survived slapped fresh carbon magazines into their pulse rifles and moved forward.

Ajax saw that Ford had either passed out or died, and did not have the time to check. The marine was out of the fight, and for now that was all that mattered. Moments later they reached the edge of the boulder field, and Sharif gestured for a halt.

"First wave in position!" announced Sharif through the company channel when they reached their destination.

"Second wave advance!" responded Jarl Mahora. "Shieldwall on my order. Check your downrange and minimize friendly fire casualties. We are about to tighten the noose."

Ajax crouched behind a small boulder, sweeping his vision through the iron sights of his rifle back and forth across the open ground around the stone tower. Recon data indicated that there were at least two sea cave entrances at the base of the tower, and Ajax was beyond certain that their true prey awaited them in those twisted watery depths. Hydra Company had suffered mightily to secure the beachhead, such was the fate of all first waves in an assault on a secured position. Soon the marines of Gorgon Company would finish moving through the debris field, and assuming their advance upon the tower was a success, they would then be reinforced by Manticore Company.

"Getting that special feeling, Bloodhound?" asked Rama as the sound of the armored boots of Gorgon marines grew near.

"I've been buzzing since we made planetfall," answered Ajax, flexing his fingers on the rifle's grip. He hated the nickname, though sadly it had become rather appropriate. The knowledge of his 'gift' had spread quickly through the ranks of the task force, and it had not taken long for the marines to dub him with the moniker.

"I'm surprised they're holding back," observed Sharif, "There must be at least one or two Wargarm down there holding the swarms on a tight leash, else they'd have come at us by now."

"There's something worse than a Wargarm down there, brother," Ajax assured his comrades as the Gorgon marines reached their position, each man among them carrying the interlocking mobile flak boards that would allow them to advance with some modicum of protection.

"Another Grendel," said a Gorgon marine with a jovial tone that was rather out of place amidst the piles of bodies and broken stones as he marched up to Ajax, the name Jorah stenciled upon his chest plate. "We'll get you to those caves, Bloodhound, just save a piece of that monster for the rest of us, okay?"

Ajax nodded his thanks and turned back towards the open ground before them. Most of the marines outside Hydra Company did not know Ajax by his face, though he had his name stenciled on his armor like every other marine. The tale of his dance with Grendel across several battles on Heorot had become something of legend amongst the marines of the task force.

His ability to focus his awareness of the garm was not sufficiently strong for him to hunt down an individual alien, it was more impressions and sensations. He felt less like a bloodhound and more like a fortune teller, honestly, though it gave the marines a morale boost to think of him as having powers more precise. The skalds and jarls had insisted that he not take steps to divest the marines of that illusion, so yet again, Ajax found himself compelled to maintain a level of secrecy from his battle brothers. It cost him something to nod his thanks, but it was a price that had to be paid.

"Second wave in position," said Jorah over the company channel. "On you, Mahora."

"Shieldwall!" bellowed the jarl and as one, the marines of Gorgon Company stepped out from behind cover and began locking their flak boards together to form the armored infantry wall.

Ajax felt his heart pounding in his chest like a drum as the impressive line of marines advanced. As the Gorgon marines cleared the boulder field, the remaining Hydra marines fell in behind them. Their boots crunching on the rocky ground as they marched.

The wall had moved only a few meters towards the tower when the enemy responded with extreme prejudice.

PHALANX

Ajax involuntarily sucked in his breath as the swarm of gorehounds erupted from several depressions at the base of the tower, presumably entrances to the vast sea cave network described in the Kai Prime briefing.

No matter how many times he stood against the garm, the gorehounds in particular were a troublesome opponent to face without some degree of nausea present. The hideous creatures were essentially living guns that galloped on cloven-hooves, and when they achieved range their weapons were more horrifying yet.

The marine in front of Ajax began firing the second the gorehounds came into range. For what it was worth, the marines would have a few precious moments of free fire before the enemy's weapons achieved their own range.

Jorah held his shield in above the first marine and locked it into place alongside the men to his left and right. It was a solid wall of flak board, each shield offering a firing port for the marines who crouched low.

Ajax marched just behind the two men, the marine himself forming the supporting line. If the marine in front died and fell, it was Jorah's job was to assume the crouching position and Ajax would then step into the covering position Jorah had just vacated.

To fight on open ground like this, to advance against an enemy such as the garm, was a guarantee that the conflict would be little more than a bloody grind. The Einherjar were betting that they could best the enemy in what appeared to be a war of attrition, a situation usually favoring the garm.

The marine formations started opening up across the island. Soon the thunder of dozens of pulse rifles hurling plasma at the alien menace gave Ajax a measure of strength. It was a small thing, a lessening of the exhaustion as even more adrenaline flooded his system, but it was significant in its effect. No amount of combat drugs could compare to the thrill of righteously unleashing violent death upon a deserving opponent. Ajax flexed his fingers on his rifle and very nearly felt guilty about his burning desire to get into the fight, as doing so would mean that at least one of the men in front of him had been slain and left a place for him to take.

For a moment, Ajax considered shoving Jorah and the other marine out of the way so that he could get a clean shot at the enemy. Darker thoughts threatened to bubble up into his consciousness, anger that men stood between him and the nightmare creatures and Ajax had to shake his head to clear them from his mind. That was the black trying to swallow him, and he could not give it any space in his thoughts. To steady himself Ajax placed a hand on Jorah's shoulder.

The advancing marine did not seem to notice the gesture, as it was a common enough movement when marines stacked up to assault an objective. Ajax kept his head down and focused on his breathing as the formation pushed forward. No sense in working himself up until it was his turn to fight, for now he just had to keep putting one foot in front of the other. He could hear the screams of dying gorehounds as the marines poured on the damage, and within seconds, the man in front paused in his fusillade to vent the heat of his rifle.

Just before the marine was able to return to his work, his shield, and much of the rest of those held by the front line, bucked wildly as the gorehounds found their range.

Hundreds of tiny grubs impacted against the flak board as the marine did his best to hold it up against the attack. Ajax knew that many of the grubs would simply splatter against the surface of the shield, though a certain number of them would survive the initial collision. Those few survivors would feed voraciously upon the shield, literally chewing their way through the hard material and gorging themselves to the point of exploding.

Luckily, the shield held, even if just barely, and the marine returned fire. From the screams, he heard on both sides of him, Ajax knew that several of the other marines on the front had not been so blessed. As the formation marched forward, he cast his glance up and down the line and saw the broken and twisted bodies of marines being left behind on the broken ground.

A shout of pain snapped Ajax's sight back to the marine in front of him just in time to see the shield collapse under the pressure of a second salvo from the gorehounds.

The marine's body shuddered as dozens of grubs rapidly burrowed through his body armor. He dropped his rifle and the remnants of his shield as he fell on his back. Without pause, Jorah lowered his shield while still marching and crouched as he began squeezing the trigger of his pulse rifle. Ajax slung the flak board off of his shoulder and raise it over his head while stepping around the writhing marine. As Ajax moved past him, the fallen marine's body jerked violently as the few grubs that had managed to chew through his armor to reach flesh, exploded from their meal, and Ajax knew that if the feeding didn't kill the man, the wet detonations certainly would.

Ajax slotted his shield into place just above Jorah, and almost immediately he had to brace himself against the force of another barrage of grub rounds from the swarm.

"Top line, full auto in two breaths!" boomed the voice of Jarl Mahora, and Ajax sucked in the first breath as he selected full auto on his rifle.

At the second breath, he lifted his shield up just enough to set the barrel of his rifle on the top of Jorah's shield. Ajax squeezed the trigger, pulling down on his shield while Jorah pushed up, keeping the weapon from kicking out of position. Ajax could not see what he was shooting at, the tactic was more about buying Jorah and the other marines in his position time to either vent their rifles or swap out carbon magazines.

They were advancing even as the garm rushed towards them, and there would be precious little time to keep up the shooting before the battle devolved into close quarters, a situation which vastly favored the garm. Even gorehounds that had expended all of their grub sacks were still equipped with razor sharp hooves and teeth as long as a man's finger.

Ajax's pulse rifle roared as it hurled round after round into the thick press of alien bodies. They were so close now that the risk of friendly fire was negligible as bolts tore through the tight ranks of the enemy. Though Ajax could not see the gorehounds, the sound of their bestial screams and the cacophony of their messy deaths made it clear that the swarm was almost upon them. Likely it would be this close across the entire battlefront. They were taking a gamble attacking this way, and Ajax could only hope that the skald's plan would bear fruit before the marine formation was shattered by close quarters contact.

His weapon seized up just as the magazine went empty, and Ajax knew that even if he vented the excess heat and put in a new magazine it would be several moments before the weapon would be ready to fire again. Going full auto was as desperate as it was devastating, and Ajax slung his rifle the moment it stopped firing. He slid his side arm out of the holster on his hip and thumbed off the safety.

It had been a long time since he'd used a pistol in battle against the garm, usually the fighting was done or he was dead before such holdout weapons found their use. The pistols were not overly effective, even though they were smaller versions of the pulse rifles, as they had drastically less stopping power. He knew as the grip filled his hand that the pistol would be good for maybe one kill if he was lucky, before it either over heated or he was torn to pieces.

Another mighty volley of grub rounds crashed against the shieldwall as the surviving gorehounds responded, and both Jorah and Ajax struggled to keep their shields in place. The moment after impact, Ajax pitched his ruined shield over his shoulder and raised his pistol.

Jorah had already discarded his own shield and was venting his pulse rifle while taking a knee. The formation had halted across the battlefront. Most of the marines had lost their shields and were preparing for a grisly death in melee with the garm.

Ajax could see the corpse littered ground ahead. The gorehound swarm, while nearly wiped out, still had enough strength to make the marines pay dearly for their advance.

As he raised his pistol and filled his sights with the enemy, the psychic pressure of the garm exploded within his mind. He was nearly forced to his knees as the Wargarm emerged from the base of the tower.

He could feel them in his mind, and they were enraged.

The Wargarm were not sentient in the classic sense, though they were much more advanced organisms than the cannon fodder that comprised the bulk of the garm swarms. The multitude of hideous creatures that comprised the extinction fleet were simple beings, running on genetic programming and raw instinct.

The Wargarm functioned in a way, like squad leaders, to Ajax's thinking, in that they could exert what the Einherjar now knew was a sort of psychic control over the lesser garm organisms. At first, it was thought this swarm hierarchy was a chemical relationship, and while it could still have that component, the fighting on Heorot, and Ajax's own bond with the Wargarm hybrid known as Grendel, indicated a deep psychic connection among the alien invaders.

Ajax knew when the three Wargarm appeared, that they were desperate to defend whatever was down in those caves. The Wargarm might still have only a simple intellect when it came to modern combat, but they were not the relentless attackers that the other swarms were.

Wargarm had proven themselves capable of modest tactical decisions like disengaging from conflict, taking cover to avoid being gunned down and, ever since those first engagements on Heorot, the capacity to single out individual marines for slaughter instead of simply attacking whoever was closest.

Ajax prepared for death as the Wargarm and the handful of gorehounds that remained prepared to attack. Then he heard the roar of engines that held a slim promise of survival.

"*Edda Five*, engaging!" announced the familiar voice of Skald Omar as the special forces gunship streaked over the heads of the embattled marines on the island.

The gunship *Edda Five* had been seconded to the task force and given a berth upon *Bright Lance*. While the marine legions of the Einherjar typically enjoyed modest air support in the form of Ravens, which were small one-man craft that sported a mounted pulse rifle, those were typically used for recon. Long ago, the forces of humanity had learned the hard way that any air support committed to the field would have to contend with the suicidal shrieker swarms that would hurl themselves into every engine port or propeller blade they could.

Ajax recalled early in the war, watching a gunship just like *Edda Five* explode in midair when shriekers flew themselves through the thruster intake vents. As with the other garm organisms, the shriekers carried their ammunition within their own bodies, so when the internal organs containing their caustic projectiles were destroyed, that ammo all but dissolved the gunship's vital systems.

Like their pulse rifles, their resurrection, and their skill with trench warfare, the Einherjar and the forces of humanity had to adapt. Fighting without an offensive air force was something men like Ajax had been doing for years.

The sight of the gunship filled the marines with elation, and a howl of bloodlust and victory went up among the Einherjar as the ship engaged the garm. The *Edda Five* was equipped with twin chainfires mounted just under its mid-section, which bellowed as they spewed hundreds of super-heated bolts scything through the enemy. Gorehounds exploded everywhere as the gunner marked his range and began to sweep the barrels of the weapon towards the Wargarm.

Ajax pumped his fist in the air and shouted as he witnessed one of the Wargarm impaled by an eight-foot-long spike launched from one of the tubes mounted under the gunship's stubby L-shaped wings. They were called javelins, which seemed a fitting name, as they were little more than finely crafted spears that were launched with compressed air from the ship. They were specifically designed to kill Ultragarm, and although they saw little use due to the shrieker swarms, they were still effective when they were finally deployed.

"Work's not done, marines! Let's finish this fight!" shouted Jarl Mahora over the company channel, his gruff voice snapping Ajax out of his reverie at the majesty of the gunship.

While the plan had been to make a daring assault that was so aggressive that the Wargarm were drawn out of hiding, which seemed to have worked, there were still plenty of gorehounds either active or wounded on the battlefront.

Ajax took aim at one of the creatures and began methodically punching its thick hide with pistol bolts. By the time the beast collapsed in a wet heap, Ajax had to slide in his second and last carbon mag. Jorah was faring better with his pulse rifle and brought down two more gorehounds with cold precision.

The *Edda* turned its full arsenal against the remaining two Wargarm and made short work of the beasts. Nobody wanted to fight those monsters in the tight confines of the sea caves, and it would have cost as many, if not more, marine lives than the entire assault up to this point. Better to risk losing two thirds of their forces on the island surface and hitting the Wargarm with a gunship than to make a tactical insertion closer to the base of the tower and be forced to fight the swarm leaders inside what everyone presumed was their hive.

Jorah stepped aside and gave the thrashing form of a wounded gorehound a wide berth, leaving Ajax to shoot it in the head. Ajax usually took little pleasure in the grisly work of killing the wounded, something of the warrior in him preferring the stand-up fight of it all.

However, as Ajax looked down the iron sights of his pistol, he found himself equally elated to play the role of executioner. Any kill was a good kill, he found himself thinking, and it wasn't until he saw Jorah looking at him that he realized he'd said it out loud.

"Rally on the tower and pull security, nothing gets out alive and nobody goes in!" ordered Jarl Mahora, and for the first time that day, Ajax could see the grim marine leading a group of beleaguered Gorgon marines across the heaps of corpses towards the tall rock formation "Manticore, hit the beachhead and advance to rally point. You still alive out there, Bloodhound?"

"Ajax online, sir," responded the marine as he vented the heat of his pistol before holstering it so that he could reload his pulse rifle.

"Good to hear," snarled Mahora, "You're going in with the blackouts."

A WATERY GRAVE

Ajax watched his fallen friend, Boone, shake with rage as the minders held him fast with their poles, the tip of each one fastened to a swift-release collar that allowed them to control the blackout. The man's fists clenched and unclenched in anticipation of release, the sounds he was making garbled by the muzzle they'd put inside the man's helmet.

Blackouts were known to speak endlessly about the violence they wanted to do to the garm, and though the aliens were the enemy, it was a truly haunting phenomenon to witness.

The blood lust became so great that when a marine 'blacked out' his mind was all but consumed with the thirst for war and violence against the alien enemy.

Boone was no different, and Ajax could see that the man was barely restrained. It was only the combination of the minders and the knowledge that he was about to be released into enemy territory that kept the berserker even moderately manageable.

Ajax missed Boone, and though he knew little of the man, like so many of his other friends, there had been some spark of a connection. The thought of his band of brothers made Ajax look around him, and his eyes fell on Sharif and Rama, the only two grunts to survive the ground assault. Somewhere behind them were the savaged bodies of Ford, Silas, and Yao, each of them destined to be reborn days later in the body forge.

Hart too had survived the assault, as Ajax had spotted him speaking with Skald Omar once the gunship landed to deploy several of the special forces operators. Ajax had not seen much of the enigmatic sniper, though given the warrior's new place amongst the skald ranks, it made sense that the man would live and work somewhat apart from the rank and file infantry. Ajax might be the Bloodhound these days, but he was still a grunt. Despite his newfound abilities, those in command, from Jarl Mahora to Skald Wallace and his advisors, insisted that he remain part of Hydra Company. Considering how easily he could have been killed during the ground assault and yet how critical Skald Omar seemed to think his individual decisions might be, there had to be some deeper stratagem at work behind the decision to allow Ajax to remain a simple rifle. For the most part, he was fine with that, trusting in his jarl and command to wage war as they saw fit. It was the secret keeping that he vehemently detested, though orders were orders, and he was nothing if not a soldier and servant of the All-Father.

"Ajax, you're up," said Jarl Mahora as he marched up to Ajax and his comrades, "Once I release the blackouts we give it a three count and you advance with squads from Manticore."

"I'm ready," said Ajax as Skald Omar approached from behind the jarl and held up a small datapad.

"We've identified three points of ingress to the sea caves," stated the skald as he brought up a three-dimensional image of the caves with each of the entrances highlighted, "After the ground assault we are right at half strength. Gorgon Company took a beating to be sure, but Hydra Company is down to a handful of men. Manticore is fresh and spoiling for a fight, so we'll put them at the vanguard of the cave ops. We need you to tell us where to put you."

"We'll drop a hell of a hammer into the other two caves, but you know as well as we do that the one you pick is the prime target," growled Mahora, "Whatever is down there ain't gonna die easy, but if it's you that finds it then that's more weight behind this whole Norse saga theory Command is playing with."

"While your jarl may be skeptical, Ajax," snapped Omar as he looked sideways at Mahora, "The skalds are not. Thanes we can send into all three entrances, but our Beowulf must choose his ground, and once you do, I have no doubt that there you will meet our monster."

"Jormungandr," scoffed Mahora, "Another beast from your stories."

"Grendel was real enough, sir," observed Hart as he joined the group, "I remain skeptical myself, though if we indeed find a relative of the beast here on Kai Prime, the evidence in favor of Skald Omar's hypothesis would mount significantly."

"Well let's get on with it then. Even if it's just a bunch more Wargarm down there they still need purging," grumbled Mahora before speaking over the command channel, "Marines in position! Blackouts on the ready line!"

Ajax shared a nod with Hart and then went to take his place a few steps behind Boone. The minders were having a harder time controlling him now that it was clear the violence was about to begin. A third minder approached Boone and Ajax could see that the man held the auto-pistol and sharp sword that were the iconic weapons of the blackout berserkers.

Ajax squared his shoulders and took in a deep breath as nearly one hundred marines took up positions behind him. According to the briefing, they were to enter the cave in waves, just like the ground assault, moving in loose squads of ten men at a time. The chemical makeup of the stone and coral were expected to interfere with short range communications, so it was unlikely that once inserted the fire teams would have much contact with each other over the company channel. Jarl Mahora wanted to stagger the insertion just in case any sort of counter-attack appeared on the surface, while still ensuring that they could fill the sea cave network with rifles.

Rama and Sharif shouldered their way past several Manticore marines, seemingly determined to stay by the side of their comrade. Ajax knew better than to insist that they did not need to be on the front line again after fighting so relentlessly to seize the beachhead. The men of Manticore did not protest, nor did those of Gorgon, as Hydra Company had earned itself something of a reputation after the conflict on Heorot. It made sense to the marines that warriors from Hydra would be at the tip of the spear. There was something of a poetic rightness to it, so much so that Ajax found himself even more suspicious that Skald Omar and his followers might be right about narrative stratagems. Unless, he realized, it was Hart who was correct, and they were on some journey of self-fulfilling prophecy. Ajax smiled to himself at the fact that Jarl Mahora would insist that it didn't matter so long as a sufficient amount of garm ass was kicked.

Boone stood in front of Ajax, shifting his weight from one foot to the other as he flexed his shoulders and hefted the weight of pistol and sword. This was Boone's first engagement as a blackout, and Ajax found himself wondering if there was enough left of the man he knew for Boone to be aware of the novelty.

With a shout from the jarl, whether it was the first time for Boone or not ceased to matter, as the minders released their hold on the berserkers.

For an instant, Ajax felt the psychic pressure of the enemy swell, a marked difference from the relative absence once the Wargarm had been slain, and he knew that something was preparing itself for the coming fight.

Boone surged forward, no doubt screaming himself raw into the muzzled helmet, and rushed into the darkness of the cave entrance.

The hole was sizeable, the aperture large enough for a tank to drive through, and it was only the near horizontal position of it at the bottom of a dip on the rock that had made it difficult to see from a surface perspective.

Ajax took a deep breath and began tapping his finger against the metal of his pulse rifle just above the trigger guard, counting out five taps before letting his air out and taking another breath. Before he'd released the second breath the shooting began somewhere down in the caves as the other fire teams engaged the enemy. He could both hear the screams of dying beasts and feel their passing in the shadowy depths of his consciousness.

Ajax sucked in his third breath, dug in his heels, and then launched himself into a sprint as he let it out. The marine's low lumen body lights generated an ambient glow in the tunnel as he ran, and the light mounted on his pulse rifle cast a tight beam that sliced through the gloom ahead.

He had only run for a few moments before he began splashing through salty water that got deeper with every few steps he took. It wasn't long until Ajax was wading in water up to his waist. If this continued he and the rest of the marines would have to activate their re-breathers.

The Einherjar had a variety of armor upgrades that could be toggled depending upon the needs of the environment. The aquatic upgrades were simple enough, as each marine had mesh webbing between their fingers and their re-breathers had been fitted with small ox canisters. The canisters were good for roughly an hour, and Ajax was happy to have the upgrades, as there was no telling just how much further down the caves went.

Soon the thunderous sounds of combat erupted inside the tunnel, and the marines rushed towards it as the tunnel opened up into a larger chamber with a multitude of side tunnels and several large rock outcroppings. Boone stood in the center of the chamber, firing wildly down one of the tunnels, the water around him churning with unidentifiable carnage. Already, the berserker appeared to have sustained a number of grievous wounds, though his rage would carry him through for at least a short time more. As Ajax emerged from the tunnel he witnessed the waves crashing as something large moved just beneath the surface of the water towards the berserker.

Ajax raised his rifle to fire just as the beast launched itself out of the water towards Boone. Ajax hesitated for a split second, his eyes and his mind filled with the sight of the nightmare creature. It was a garm unlike any he had seen before, which in itself added to the mental shock.

It had the overall appearance of a ripper drone, though its body appeared to have been radically adapted to an aquatic environment. It had webbing across its armpits and between its claws, and a spined dorsal fin ran from the base of its skull to the bottom of its spine. The eyes were different, larger, and bulbous somehow, the sight of it reminded him of the angler fish that often resided in the crushing depths of ancient oceans. It kicked off with what Ajax could only presume were webbed feet, launching itself at the berserker with claws and scything blades bristling for the kill.

Boone, however, did not hesitate, when the beast's lunge brought it within striking distance, the berserker made his move.

As the drone roared and brought its limbs down towards him, the blackout spun on his heels and lashed out with his greatsword. The sharp blade cleaved the beast neatly in two. Before the pieces had sunk beneath the dark waters, Boone raised his pistol and pointed it at the marines who were at the tunnel entrance.

Ajax's blood turned to ice in his veins, as it looked like Boone was about to turn his fearsome weapon upon his comrades, then, as the berserker squeezed the trigger, a scream of pain from above said otherwise. The bloody corpse of a ripper splashed into the water in front of Ajax and snapped the marine out of his shock at the sight of new garm organisms.

The garm adapt.

Marines overcome.

More drones came howling out of the various side tunnels, and Ajax, along with Rama and Sharif, took a knee and began squeezing off rounds. Manticore marines shouldered their rifles and fired over the heads of their kneeling comrades, lending six or more pulse rifles to the fight.

The drones poured out of the tunnels, all seemingly fixated on the blackout, the nearest and most obvious threat.

Despite the marine's punishing fire, for every ripper they blasted, another splashed into the water and jetted towards the berserker.

Boone stood at the center of the watery chamber, his pistol discarded, and swung his greatsword with a two- handed grip. The berserker was fast, though not as fast as the garm horrors, but he was precise in his movements, and beast after beast fell to his blade.

Ajax thanked the stars that the lower garm swarms were so single-minded in their assault. They were so focused upon Boone that the majority of them ignored the marines fire team.

Ajax paused to vent the heat from his rifle, and as he did so, he witnessed one of the rippers slip under Boone's slicing blade. Before the berserker could step aside or bring the sword around for a parry, the garm's own bio-blades tore through armor and flesh. No sooner had the first spilled blood, then another emerged from under the waves and impaled Boone through the back. In the blink of an eye the mighty slayer disappeared beneath the churning waters.

"*Push in!*" shouted Sharif, taking charge of the firefight now that one of their own was no longer downrange.

The marines behind and above Ajax paused in their firing to allow the crouching men to stand and press into the chamber. Soon marines were rushing into the battlespace faster and in more numbers than the garm.

Ajax fired ten rounds in rapid succession into the water near where Boone had been taken, and the plasma bolts filled the watery chamber with steam as they vaporized the gory liquid. Next to him, Rama followed suit, and the marines were rewarded by the sight of a thrashing and dying pair of drones that came to the surface.

Ajax vented the heat of his rifle and cast his sight around the chamber, realizing that it was significantly larger than he'd thought. He looked up and could see the tiny rays of light from Kai Sol, the solar body that gave light and life to the system, cutting through the darkness above.

They found themselves in the main chamber beneath the tower. Ajax readied his rifle again and fired three times in rapid succession to end the life of a ripper drone that attempted to crawl out of a side tunnel above them and drop down into the melee. The drones kept coming, but in smaller and smaller numbers, until soon they came no more.

The engagement had been more of a slaughter than a battle, but the marine force had not escaped unscathed. The sheer number of drones combined with their suicidal ferocity had indeed claimed a handful of Einherjar, though the tactic of sending the blackout in first and the vantage point of the tunnel that turned the chamber into a shooting gallery had heavily favored the marines.

There wasn't enough room in the chamber for the several score of marines who had come this way, and though they could hear the thunderous echoes of other fire teams elsewhere in the cave system no doubt facing similar battles, these tunnels needed exploring. It was difficult to move through the chamber, as the water was now clogged with bodies.

"This place just became a death trap, mobility is null, and I'm not getting anything on the company channel. First team, pull security!" said a marine with the name Quinn stenciled across his chest. Ajax recognized him as one of the defacto Manticore leaders, functioning much like Sharif did when Jarl Mahora wasn't around. "Lead on, Ajax. Pick your tunnel and we'll stack you with a full platoon. The rest of us will fan out and purge the rest of the hive."

"By the gods, this is a hive!" breathed Rama as he swept his gaze across the chamber and upwards into the ancient vent.

"You are such a grunt," groaned Sharif, rolling his eyes, but smiling.

Ajax turned from the three marines as the other warriors scrambled to secure the entrances to the side tunnels that were level with the bottom of the chamber while others aimed their rifles up to cover those that were out of reach.

The marine began to control his breathing, and slowly worked to clear his mind with the meditation techniques the skalds had been teaching him. The psychic pressure was there, though now it was more of a delicate pulse than anything. Rather than fading though, the pulse was a small and growing thing, as if it was slowly building itself up in his mind. It was not the explosive rage he'd felt earlier, no, this was something more juvenile, a hunger without malice, and yet, that hunger already had the bottomless sensation that threatened to swallow him every time he got too close to the Hive Mind. The trick was engaging with that psychic pressure but not allowing it to gain too much of a foothold in his consciousness.

He reached out with his awareness, his eyes closed, and focused on the pulse. His hard-won gift did not tell him which tunnel to take, it had never been anywhere near that precise, though he did begin to feel a pull in the general direction of left and down. The marine gently turned his body to face where he felt the pulse, not allowing his other senses to create static, purging himself of as much incoming data that wasn't the psychic pulse as he could.

Ajax slowly opened his eyes and looked in front of him.

He was standing at the mouth of a side tunnel. He felt it more than he knew it, that down that passage lay whatever nightmare they'd come to find. Disturbing as these mutated ripper drones might have been, the real horror was further down. Ajax squared his shoulders and took a step towards the tunnel, prompting Sharif and Rama to fall in behind him.

"Second team, on me, third team break out into squads and start securing the lower tunnels. Watch out for friendly fire, the other fire teams are going to be wandering around as blindly as we are," ordered Quinn as he began directing scores of troops who moved with some difficulty through the corpse clogged waters to fall into their formations.

As the marines struggled to cross the chamber and enter the tunnels, Ajax himself pushed past several floating bodies to reach the tunnel he was positive led to the goal of this mission. What that might be, he could not say, whether it was another monster like Grendel, this Jormungandr that Omar and Hart spoke of, or something worse.

THE CLUTCH

The growing hunger built up pressure in his consciousness as Ajax entered the tunnel. He'd only gone a few meters before the psychic residue of the dead and dying ripper drones had been completely replaced by that hunger. The water got deeper, and soon the marines were up to their chest. Their submerged body lights gave the water an unearthly glow that in any other circumstance might have been considered beautiful.

After several more meters the tunnels began to splinter off, some going straight down and others angling upwards. It was becoming more and more difficult for Ajax to sift through the waves of sensation he was getting from whatever garm horror lay in wait for them.

"Contact right!" shouted Sharif suddenly as he turned and began firing.

Ajax bent his knees slightly, fully submerging his head in the water of the tunnel and saw in the eerie glow that they'd moved into another small chamber. Most of the new tunnels led further down and unless they'd been looking for it they could easily have fallen down one of the handful of openings large enough to swallow a man whole. For what it was worth, Ajax found that he could see much better under the water than he could above it, something about the sheen of the light against the surface of the rocks.

The marine saw Sharif squeezing the trigger of his pulse rifle and a hurricane of bubbles and billowing steam rose as his plasma bolts streaked through the water and impacted against the thick hide of a ripper drone. While Sharif pounded one attacker, another surged upwards out of a hole in the chamber floor.

Before Ajax could level his weapon at it, the beast wrapped its claws around the legs of a marine, jamming a bio-blade through the man's thigh. Ajax watched helplessly through his iron sights as the marine disappeared into the hole, dragged down by the garm. Another emerged from a side tunnel entrance, heading straight for Rama, only this time both he and Ajax were ready. Their combined fire filled the chamber with steam and carnage as the beast flailed in death.

Ajax was about to squeeze the trigger and slay another when he was yanked off his feet by something below him. He looked down to see that a ripper drone had dug its claws into the armor of his left leg. Instantly, it sped downwards, smashing Ajax into the floor of the chamber before dragging him across the rough surface, into a deeper part of the chamber towards one of the fully submerged holes. Ajax scrambled for purchase with his left hand, desperately clinging to his pulse rifle with his right, knowing in the chaos that his comrades would not have seen him go down, too busy defending themselves from the sudden close quarters assault.

The garm disappeared down the hole and in the last second before he, too, went down, Ajax quit grabbing rocks with his left hand and gripped the pulse rifle with both hands. The garm wasn't expecting the resistance, so when the rifle slammed into place across the mouth of the hole, smashing the mounted light, the alien beast lost its grip on the marine. Ajax knew his left leg had been savaged, and he'd lost some of the armor there, but the pain meant he still had a leg, and that was something at least. He kicked his legs fast and hard pulling himself up on his rifle.

No sooner had he escaped the hole than another drone slid through the water above him towards his comrades. Without thinking, he ripped the trench spike from his belt and thrust it upwards. The momentum of the beast and his own sudden fury drove the point hilt-deep just under the beast's chin. Ajax pulled himself up using the handle and pressed his feet against the drone's chest.

He knew that despite the garm's tiny brain being pierced the beast was still dangerous and he needed to get clear of it. He wrenched the spike free of the wound, simultaneously pushing off the creature's chest, sending himself down while sending the thrashing monster up to the surface. Ajax smacked into the rock floor of the chamber and rolled over quickly to wrap his fingers around the grip of his pulse rifle.

He let out a shout of victory that quickly died in his throat as the ripper that had first grabbed him lashed out from just inside the hole. One of its bio-blades buried itself in the gap in the marine's armor where forearm met elbow. In an instant Ajax was pulled down the hole and dragged into darkness.

Without his body lights, he had no idea beyond the rush of water which way was even up. Ajax fought through the pain and forced his finger to squeeze the trigger repeatedly. The first round must have gone wide, as the drone kept swimming down, it was impossible to tell for sure in the rush of vaporized water from the plasma discharge. His second shot, and perhaps even his third, were enough to end the creature.

The drone released its grip on Ajax a moment after they entered a fully submerged chamber. As the bloody corpse floated past him in charred pieces, Ajax could see the low, sloping walls of the chamber and decided it was much larger than even the first they'd seen. His body lights created a soft orb of light around him that extended out several meters. He knew he was seeing only a fraction of the interior. Regardless of what he could and could not see, the marine was filled with absolute certainty that he'd found what they were looking for.

The psychic pall of hunger buffeted against him, and the marine fumbled with his flare in a desperate attempt to have light. He pointed one flare upwards and shot it back into the hole he'd come from, hoping that the others had survived the ambush and could follow him down. He aimed the other into the darkness and fired.

Seconds later he wished that he hadn't, some things could not be unseen.

The green light of the flare bathed the large chamber in a glow that clearly illuminated the abomination that occupied its center. The walls were curved in the way one would expect of a cave formed by volcanic activity as opposed to the more jagged caves made by the endless motion of waves. Ajax could see a veritable forest of active stacks, each one the size of a small tree, belching super-heated minerals into the briny water of the cave. The sight of that alone might have given a man pause, but it was the presence of the alien menace that twisted the marine's guts.

What he could only assume were clutches of egg sacks had been affixed to the vents throughout the stone forest. They clustered like barnacles around the vents, the larger ones at the base and the smaller ones near the top. As he watched in horror he realized that the smaller ones took in nutrients, and as they grew they slid down the vent to the base, where they hatched. He swung his rifle in a wide arc to cover the room as he looked down his sights to see that the floor of the chamber was completely obscured by what had to be hundreds, if not thousands, of hatched and discarded eggs.

More than even that nightmarish sight, what drew his eye and his aim was the pool near the largest of the vents. Whatever amniotic fluids were present in the pool had a different atomic weight than the rest of the water in the cave, as it remained contained within the pool.

While there was no garm organism in the pool presently, he recognized it for what it was. He had been aboard Grendel's hive ship, and he knew that he was looking upon the brood home of the beast that Command and the skalds had taken to calling Jormungandr.

As the realization struck him, something moving below his position caught his attention. He shifted his aim towards what appeared to be a giant snail-like creature moving among the smoking stacks. It was pressing a proboscis from the front of its body into the smaller egg sacks, filling them with some manner of fluid from its own body. Before Ajax had time to process that particular horror the dull thud of weapons fire reached his ears.

He was sinking fast, the weight of his armor pulling him down towards the heaps of hatched eggs. Without any propulsion system, there was little he could do but kick hard to ensure he landed on solid stone.

The company channel still bled static, and he could not even fully make out the garbled voices of his comrades a mere level above. These mineral rich sea caves might be a perfect breeding ground, but they severely disrupted conventional communication networks.

Ajax had to wonder whether or not that had been a factor in the garm brood choosing this place. There were thousands of such formations throughout the watery planet, so picking this one to assault was truly the finding of a needle in a haystack, as the saying went.

More gunfire echoed thunderously off the thick walls of the cave, and a sudden increase in the psychic pressure brought the marine's attention to a small tunnel opening ahead and above him. Several thick tentacles with large suckers slid out of the darkness of the entrance and were soon followed by a beast so hideous the marine's mind struggled to cope with the sight.

It was serpentine, much like Grendel had been on Heorot, though where Grendel was clearly a creature adapted to land, this one appeared to have been born for a primarily aquatic existence.

It had the same cockroach-meets-reptile visage as the other garm broods, though in place of the scything blades of Grendel, reminiscent of the ripper drones, this nightmare sported undulating tentacles, each of which ended in a barbed tip.

As it cleared the confines of the tunnel, the creature folded its tentacles tight against its body and streaked through the water to splash into the viscous amniotic pool.

Briefly, Ajax thought it had not noticed him, despite his body lights and their apparent psychic connection, but no sooner had the surface of the pool grown calm than it erupted with waves again as the beast rose from its depths.

The reflective black eyes of Jormungandr locked with those of Ajax as the marine's boots crunched through the shells of hatched eggs and came to rest upon the stony floor.

The beast's dark eyes flashed impossibly with recognition, and the dull ache of the psychic pressure suddenly jabbed into Ajax's mind like a spike.

Ajax snapped his rifle to his shoulder and tried to squeeze the trigger, only to discover that his armored digit would not obey his command. The pain in his mind moved to his hands and he felt with all certainty that Jormungandr was exerting control over his body. Even Grendel did not have that power, else it would have done more against him when he and Boone had finished it off. The hesitation lasted but a moment as Ajax powered through the psychic wall put in his way and forced his finger to apply pressure to the pulse rifle's trigger.

The moment the pulse rifle kicked with the first salvo of super-heated bolts, Jormungandr launched itself from the healing pool. Ajax's rounds went wide as the aquatic nightmare streaked through the water. He could see the bioluminescent fluids still glowing as they worked to bind the multitude of wounds he now saw on the garm's body. He had not noticed them before the beast had submerged itself, and now here, in the half-light of the chamber, the beast named Jormungandr had clearly been in a hell of a fight. The fact that it was here with him, exchanging bolts for barbs, meant that somewhere in this cave network floated the corpses of untold scores of marines.

Ajax kicked off of the stony ground and angled his body to the left, the opposite direction he'd have gone if he'd moved on instinct, and his choice kept him alive.

At least four, perhaps more, barbed projectiles sliced through the water where he'd been standing. Jormungandr knew that much about him at least, and the thought gave Ajax the chills.

Could the Hive Mind possibly read him so accurately despite his inability to track the swarms much beyond intuition and the most basic regions on a map?

He had little time to consider such things, still squeezing the trigger as he attempted to track the aquatic beast's progress through the cave.

He knew that he was no match for the creature, and without the bracketing fire of other marines he would have little hope of achieving a clean hit, much less killing the beast. As if in answer to his plea, more jets of bubbles and vaporized water appeared in the cave as multiple green lights suddenly illuminated the entire space.

Ajax risked a glance sideways and saw Sharif, Rama, and Quinn, followed by more marines, emerging from the tunnel he'd first entered through.

Jormungandr swam low, putting the multitude of egg-crusted vents between it and the attacking marines as the cave was suddenly filled with activity.

The vents exploded as their delicate pressure was disrupted, lending their own steam and bubbles to those being created by the pulse rifles of the marines as more poured through the hole while the first arrivals sank to the floor.

A psychic howl rose from Jormungandr, buffeting Ajax with a distinct sensation of rage, and he knew without a doubt that the beast had summoned every last living garm to return to the breeding chamber.

Ajax was sickeningly positive that had he been anywhere but in the chamber already, he'd have struggled mightily to resist the call himself.

As the marines continued to wreak havoc upon the thick forest of vents, destroying eggs and stone formations in equal measure, the serpentine beast returned fire from within the growing cloud of dust, gore, and vapor.

Ajax clumsily waded through the waist deep piles of discarded eggs, doing his best to sight in on the beast, though like the others who had reached the bottom, his angle of attack was poor. Above him he saw several marines spasm violently as the ten inch barbed projectiles impaled them, punching through the gaps in their armor like miniature harpoons.

The crushing cold of the depths allowed Ajax to get twelve shots off before being required to vent rather than the traditional ten. As he worked, his view of the battlescape was temporarily obscured. Only the armor prevented him from being cooked by the sudden spike in water temperature caused by the pulse rifle.

When he looked up again, Ajax witnessed the result of Jormungandr's call for aid as dozens of the aquatically adapted ripper drones rushed into the chamber. Ajax noticed that many of them were already wounded or missing limbs, but after the first wave filled the sea cave he saw that no more attended the great beast.

This was the last gasp of a dying swarm, Ajax suddenly realized. It could only mean that Jormungandr intended to escape.

Sure enough, he saw the beast disengage from exchanging fire with the marines and flow across the base of the now much damaged vent forest. Jormungandr was no longer on the attack, or even the defense, that much Ajax knew with clarity, and he realized that he had to follow. Garm swarms never retreated, and even the higher organisms only disengaged if they were being redeployed elsewhere on the battlefield. These alpha garm were different, the likes of Grendel, and now Jormungandr.

Ajax sprinted at the best speed he could managed despite the less than ideal conditions, and by instinct, swapped out his mostly spent carbon magazine for a fresh one.

All around him the sea cave had become a roiling bloodbath as the marines fought against the remaining ripper drones. Ajax ignored them in pursuit of the great beast. He entered the vent forest and kept his rifle at the ready as his movement were suddenly hampered by the close confines.

Jormungandr would have the advantage here, given the close quarters environment, though he knew, somehow, that attack was no longer the nightmare's prime directive. It was after something in here, and he had to see it with his own eyes before either Jorumgandr was dead or achieved whatever its goal might be.

Ajax smashed several eggs with his armored shoulder as he pressed on, leaving in his wake the disgusting half-grown embryos that floated out of the broken shells.

Above and around him, garm and marine warriors tore each other to pieces. Ajax was struck more than once by sinking pieces of both drones and his comrades.

Finally, he reached the center of the vent forest, just underneath the amniotic pool, and he realized just how large it all was now that he was on the ground and not floating above it. He stepped over the discarded shell of one of the snail creatures and noticed that a brilliant green fluid seeped out of it, the atomic weight of it causing it to flow across the stony ground instead of floating in a cloud like the blood and viscera that now filled the sea cave. Had it been struck by a bolt from a pulse rifle the creature would have been reduced to chunks of gore, the marine observed as he looked at the tight holes punched in the top of the shell.

Ajax felt, more than saw, movement ahead and to the left. He raised his head, shouldering his rifle, and peered down the iron sights. His sight was filled with Jormungandr, only the beast was attacking its own kind instead of the marine. Several more shells of the snail beasts had been left at the base of the amniotic pool. As Ajax watched, Jormungandr opened its maw to punch a hardened proboscis through the shell of the snail. The bright green fluid gave a dull glow even through the proboscis as it was sucked out of the garm snail's body and into Jormungandr. Ajax saw several dully glowing sacks now bulging from the creature's thorax area.

Whatever the fluid was, the beast was removing it from the snails, which the marine recalled, the snail had been pumping into the eggs just before the melee.

Jorumgander released the dead snail and the garm's serpentine body shuddered as the glowing sacks squeezed in on themselves. Gills appeared on both sides of Jormungandr's head and the fluid poured out in thick clouds, the sacks and gills seeming to act like a sort of filter. The fluid no longer glowed, and was just a cloud of dull yellow. Ajax could not help but feel that whatever power it had before was gone. The pall of general hunger that he'd felt had faded, replaced by a bright and burning ember of rage coming specifically from the garm in front of him.

Jormungandr shuddered once more and an inky black cloud emanated from its center of mass. Ajax squeezed the trigger of his pulse rifle and sent rounds chasing the great beast, though from what he could see his rounds likely went wide. He was firing blind, but that was no reason not to continue firing. If he happened to strike a fellow marine that was an acceptable price to pay for bringing down the garm organism, and he knew that Command would so judge it.

He hit his twelve rounds and vented his gun. Ajax turned his head reflexively away from the breach, reflected in the action of the weapon he caught a glimpse of Jormungandr sliding into the entrance of a tunnel at the top of the chamber.

Ajax gathered his legs underneath him and shot up through the water after kicking off as powerfully as his legs could propel him. His aim was good and he passed through the entrance to the tunnel, muzzle first, and his body lights illuminated the rocky confines well by reflecting off the mineral deposits shining in the rock face.

Jormungandr was fleeing, he could feel it in his mind, and the marine rushed up through the tunnel without fear of sudden ambush.

It wasn't long until he began to see light, and shortly after he burst from the surface of the water to find himself on the other side of the small island.

He crawled out of the shallow water at the lip of the tunnel and took note of the thick fluid that passed for garm blood that led to the shore of the island. He stood to his full height and walked to the shore, aware of the other marines and vehicles moving around the island behind him. His company channel was ablaze with radio chatter about swarms being sighted throughout the region, all moving towards a small desalination rig, and he felt the finality of it. They had purged the hive, and the garm beast had somehow robbed them of delivering the final death blow by doing the deed itself.

Now that the breeding imperative had been removed, there was little left for the garm to do but attack. Ajax could feel the battle fury radiating from the alpha garm, mixing with his own black desires, and it filled him with a furious joy.

Jormungandr wasn't going down without a fight.

THE RIG

"It's unfortunate that whaling was never an industry that became a staple of the economy of Kai Prime," observed Skald Omar from his seat in the troop transport as it sped onwards just above the ocean's surface, "Else we might have discovered the garm incursion sooner."

"The hive was hatching its eggs using the nutrients and heat from the vents. Environmental recon suggests that the various swarms were feeding predominantly upon the weaker creatures that dove deeper in search for food," responded Hart without looking up from his work.

The sniper-turned-skald was in the process of using a fine wire brush to clean out the salt and algae deposits that appeared to have clogged much of the inner workings of his rifle. "With the garm taking over the vents, not enough of the krill that the whale feed upon were able to spawn, forcing the whales deeper and allowing them to be taken without notice."

"It does speak to a deeper understanding of ecosystems than I'd have imagined capable of the garm intellect," nodded Omar. "They achieved, with a single stroke, the feeding and care of a growing swarm and maintaining a somewhat clandestine existence by using the chain reaction to their multiple advantage. It's brilliant, really."

"So now that we've smashed up their breeding pit, what's the point in attacking a desalination rig, eh?" scoffed Mahora from his seat next to Ajax, the two men were positioned across from Omar and Hart. "Cerberus Company has reached the rig and is in the process of digging in, but I don't get what those damn bugs are trying to accomplish."

"It's the only stationary position of human civilization in this region. The nearest coastal city is halfway around the world," offered Omar, his eyes gleaming with enjoyment at the discussion.

Working out his thoughts through conversation was something Ajax had learned was a trademark with the man, much as it seemed to annoy the likes of Jarl Mahora and Skald Wallace.

"Perhaps now that their eggs have been destroyed they're reverting to a more primitive and traditional pattern of engagement? Had the events on Heorot not occurred, this would be a perfectly normal swarm tactic would it not?"

"What say you, Bloodhound?" snarled Mahora, his displeasure at the endlessly shifting tactics of the enemy naked upon his face, every ounce of him a trench fighting man. "This Jormungandr cannibalizes its own kind and then runs away as the rest of the swarms converge on the rig. You think it's going to join them, or has it gone to ground?"

"Jormungandr will be there," breathed Ajax after a few moments consideration. "I can't tell you why I know that, it's just a feeling, a certainty, actually. This doesn't feel like an attack, even if it looks like one, there's a desperation to it. More like they're racing us."

"I'm reminded of the final engagement on Heorot," said Hart, interrupting Mahora just as the jarl gathered his breath for what was likely a negative retort. "When the hive ship made a suicide run on the *Bright Lance* as swarms broke against our defenses trying to re-take Grendel's head."

"Yes, it does have the hallmarks of such a thing," agreed Omar. The skald looked out across the sea as the warning lights began to strobe, indicating that they were minutes from deployment. "Let us hope that we discover the truth of it before battle makes a mess of us all."

"The rig is automated, and only requires a crew of a dozen maintenance staff. Intel reports that they haven't completed their quarterly reporting, though the shipments of clean water have continued unabated," said Hart as the lights changed again, causing each man in the transport to double check his gear and prepare for insertion. "Perhaps the beasts were able to make use of the rig in some unknown way."

"Cerberus hasn't reported anything, but they're focused on defenses," grumbled Mahora. "Hopefully, they'll buy us enough time to get to the bottom of this. It's not like enough men walked away from that island intact to make much difference here."

Mahora's words gave Ajax cause to look up at Rama, and the marines shared a slight nod. Hyrda Company had been all but wiped out in the surprisingly costly battle for the island, and only a handful of them had emerged from the caves.

Upon reconnecting with Einherjar forces and making his report about Jormungandr's escape, Ajax had discovered that the conflict inside the caves was bloody, indeed. The other fireteams had encountered just as much resistance from the aquatic drones as the battle Ajax had been a part of.

Not only that, but Jormungandr had attacked one of the fireteams and inflicted grievous casualties before being driven away. That explained the multitude of wounds on the beast, though he still could not fathom exactly what he'd seen down in the egg chamber.

Back on Heorot, he and a number of other marines had discovered the bodies of two separate swarms of garm that had torn each other apart. In all the years of war with the aliens, such a thing was unprecedented. The garm were a colony of sorts, a great swarm controlled by whatever yet undiscovered nightmare was the source of the Hive Mind.

Ajax and his fluke of an ability merely confirmed the existence of the Hive Mind, so often theorized about by Command, though it shed little light onto the dizzying array of changes manifesting in the garm war effort.

The rig might hold some secret, and Ajax felt as if he could nearly picture what it was that Jormungandr so desperately wanted there. He knew beyond a doubt that the beast would hurl every last garm organism at the ramparts to achieve its goal, and it was nothing as simple as merely the slaughter of marines.

Cerberus Company had only been dispatched to the rig once reports of shrieker swarms moving through the sky towards it had reached Command. That new data combined with the discovery that the crew had only a few days ago missed their quarterly reporting had prompted Skald Omar and Jarl Mahora to swiftly turn the remnants of their forces around and speed towards the island.

The troop transports were moving faster this time, since each one carried a fraction of the marine bodies and gear they had only hours before at the outset of the island assault.

While some marine specialists and their attendants would stay behind to collect the priceless resurrection torcs, every rifleman and grenadier capable of carrying on the fight was ordered to rapid muster at the base of the stone tower.

Ajax was loaded down with a fresh batch of carbon magazines and a new pulse rifle, his other having been left alongside so many others to be cleaned and repaired back aboard *Bright Lance*. The combination of garm carnage, brine, and sea water had begun to give the weapons some trouble.

Sharif was no longer with them, his seat sitting empty, his torc was on its way back to the body forge. Apparently, the marine had taken several of Jormungandr's barbs to the chest and had sunk into the heaps of hatched eggs while Ajax was focused on the fighting at hand. Somewhere in the tangle of bodies, too, was Quinn, and hundreds more who had paid the price to seize the island, reach the egg chamber, and see it destroyed.

The last light strobed and the pilot pulled up on the throttle of the troop transport. Ajax leapt out of his seat and landed with a heavy thud as his boots clomped onto the slick metal grating of the rig. He saw that this particular transport had dropped its cadre of marines at the apex of the rig, a helipad platform that was centrally located. Ajax could imagine cargo and staff being loaded and unloaded here, dispersing throughout the rig from one of the tree stairwells and two open-air elevators attached to the platform. The platform was teeming with marines from Cerberus Company, who were busy bolting chainfire mounts into the decking and lashing flakboards to the rails to create firing positions for grenadiers.

As the others disembarked Ajax jogged over to the edge of the platform and held onto the railing with one hand as he peered down at the north side. The rig was a massive structure, with gangplanks and cycling cargo lines surrounding the core desalination plant like a metal and wire ribcage. Marine riflemen were positioning themselves throughout the rig, setting up hard points where they could use the mobile flak boards, though in truth there would be little cover when the garm came.

This would be a shootout.

The machine was automated, using a rotating series of gigantic buckets to gather and dump sea water into the core processor. The solar panels provided the energy for the desalinator. From what Ajax could see, the bucket-crusted wheel worked on some form of gyroscoping perpetual motion engine. As the water was purified it was dumped into plastic cargo pods that were dropped onto a belt fed cargo line that transported them to a titanic storage platform.

"Once the sensors register a target cargo weight, the entire platform detaches and uses on-board propulsion systems to follow a homing beacon back to one of the coastal cities," announced Hart as he joined Ajax at the railing. "The only real function of the staff here is to clean solar panels and scrub away salt deposits on the various gears. Neglect is why we didn't have prior warning that something was wrong here."

"The garm could have been here for months without us knowing," said Ajax as he tightened his grip on the railing, at last spotting the dark shadows of alien bodies beginning to approach on the northern perimeter.

"They have taken advantage of the neglect inherent in automated industry," nodded Hart as he took a knee and began to adjust the sights of his rifle. "Something we'll have to be aware of in the future."

"Hart has overwatch, the rest of you on me," ordered Skald Omar as he circled his finger in the air and pointed towards one of the stairwells leading down. "Jarl Mahora, you too, I am sure that Jarl Borg of Cerberus Company will have the defenses well in hand."

Ajax fell in behind Omar as the jarl, Rama, and four other marine survivors of the island assault moved to follow the skald. The tattered remnants of Gorgon and Manticore were being dropped in successive waves on the platform. As Ajax started descending the stairs he could see Jorah directing some of the troop movements alongside Borg, Gorgon's jarl having been slain back on the island.

Moving downwards, he glanced again at the north side and saw clearly that a shrieker swarm was closing in fast. He watched for a moment, stunned by what he was seeing. Soon the others did the same as they began to hear surprised chatter over the company channel. Just as the shriekers entered chainfire range, the guns opened up.

Usually, the chainfires would cut huge swathes through the flier swarms and cause bodies to rain down by the dozens. This time, the shriekers dove down to avoid the incoming barrage, and though plenty of them were still caught by the fusillade of deadly bolts, it was barely a dent in their numbers. The shriekers disappeared in the churn of the waves, diving straight down into the sea, avoiding the vast majority of the chainfire rounds.

"Brace for return fire!" shouted Jarl Borg over the company channel, and at first Ajax was confused by the man's order, though he dutifully crouched low on the staircase.

Moments later the shriekers exploded from beneath the water, having continued their advance undeterred by the water, their bodies having adapted in subtle ways to mimic the sleek design of more aquatic creatures. The shriekers were in range of their weapons, and as sooner as they returned to the air, they opened fire.

Caustic projectiles splattered across the rig as the swarm unleashed its full fury. Ajax realized just how lucky he and his squad were to be on the stairs at the moment battle was joined.

The shriekers focused their fire on the platform above, no doubt attempting to take out the devastating chainfires. In years past, the garm simply attacked the strongest opponents they could find and worked their way down. When a chainfire gunner was killed and the weapon grew silent it was subsequently ignored by the rampaging aliens.

It was upon the battlefield of Heorot that the garm tactics changed, and they appeared to acknowledge that a chainfire was a threat whether a man was using it or not, as it could come back online as soon as someone put their finger on the trigger. More than one conflict had been snatched from the jaws of defeat by a lone man bringing a chainfire online at the last moment.

While the machine guns shredded scores of shriekers, the first and second waves of projectiles from the fliers washed over the platform. The grenadiers had not been able to figure their range because of the diving tactic, so their salvo of airbursts did little but slay a handful of stragglers. The shriekers swooped up and moved in a tight arc through the air. Though the chainfires and riflemen, Ajax and Rama among them, managed to find their range and cut deep into the swarm it was able to disappear, once more, into the dark waters.

"Sling those rifles and get moving, marines!" shouted Jarl Mahora as he shouldered past Ajax, forcing the marine to grab the railing for support. "If the Skalds want us doing a sweep and clear of the interior while the rest fight and die out here, then that's what we do!"

Ajax pounded down the stairs after Mahora. The shriekers emerged once more, attempting the same swooping attack maneuver. Many more marines responded with return fire this time, and though he could hear Einherjar screaming and dying, Ajax knew that the shriekers suffered greatly.

Burning alien bodies cascaded from the sky, some smacking wetly into the network of gangplanks and cargo lines, though most splashed into the water at the base of the rig.

Skald Omar blasted the lock mechanism off of the main hatch and Jarl Mahora instantly barreled through it and into the dark. Four marines followed him, three from Manticore and one from Gorgon, as the jarl turned on his body lights and swept his gun back and forth.

"It was locked from the inside," breathed Omar, disbelievingly, while Ajax and Rama entered ahead of him, their own weapons at the ready.

The main hatch led into a common room, and Ajax knew instantly that bad things had happened there. He could see old blood stains and trashed furniture everywhere, along with deep claw marks in the metal of the far wall where something had torn through a door. On the walls were several harpoons, the jet-assisted types that sport whalers used then they wanted more of a challenge, instead of the industrial sized electro-nets of the commercial ships. One of the harpoons had been taken off the wall and actually fired, embedding itself nearly fourteen inches through the deck.

Omar knelt and observed the caked and dry gore splattered around the impact point and running up the shaft.

"They put up a fight, at least," he said as he considered the room.

Jarl Mahora grunted and shrugged his shoulders, clearly not impressed with what Omar considered putting up a fight, and moved through the interior hatch that lead down into the barracks. Ajax and the others followed him and found themselves in a small hub of sorts. There was a small elevator leading down to the desalination platform, and several hatches marked barracks, medbay, and mess hall.

These men and women lived a simple life, and for a moment Ajax wondered what that might be like, to simply toil and relax. It was, in some ways, not so different than his own, if he was honest about. This life of endless war did have a degree of tedium, and the man found himself wondering if he'd ever just relaxed and played a game of cards or billiards with his band of brothers. Such pursuits were allowed to be sure, though most men of the Einherjar kept to their training, for each ounce of sweat in training meant an ounce less blood spilled when next they met the garm upon the field.

"Down there," said Ajax suddenly, pointing to a stairwell leading down into the engineering section of the plant, his certainty a sharp blade slicing through the malaise that seemed to have fallen upon this compound.

Skald Omar and Jarl Mahora shared a look, and then the grizzled veteran shrugged and held his rifle at the ready while he began descending the stairs. Ajax fell in behind the jarl as the others took positions in the stack, each of them hugging the wall and angling their weapons downwards into the darkness. They switched on their body lights and found that the lighting had all been smashed down here, and though there was a hatch at the bottom of the stairs even the light of the buttons had been disabled.

It reminded him of the pitch dark of the sea caves, and Ajax flexed his fingers on the grip of his rifle to ease the mounting tension.

"Crack it open, lads," said Jarl Mahora as he gently tested the hatch and found it to be wedged shut even though the electronic lock had been destroyed. "I'm in first, up the center, Ajax sweep, Rama, take the right."

Two of the other marines, men from Gorgon Company, slung their rifles and produced their trench spikes. Being made of titanium with hardened points, the Einherjar trench spikes made for acceptable pry bars when needed. One man drove the point through the small seam in the hatch and heaved, giving the second marine enough space to slide his spike in and manipulate the heavy bolt that held the door shut. Had this facility been of a higher security rating there would have been over a dozen bolts in the hatch, but since it was a simple desalination plant, most of the hatches had only one bolt mechanism.

Lucky for us, thought Ajax as he thumbed off the safety of his pulse rifle and held his finger against the flat metal, just above his trigger.

As soon as the bolt was clear, the two men leapt back as Mahora drove his armored shoulder into the door, and the hatch swung inwards with a booming sound of rusted metal smacking against more rusted metal.

Ajax rushed into the darkness behind Mahora and move to the left, sweeping his pulse rifle across the sizeable engineering section, the mounted light revealing a nightmarish scene. Mahora cursed under his breath as he pounded forward and Rama gasped in surprise.

The engineering section was a large chamber outfitted with most of the technical hardware that kept the planet running. There were a multitude of vents in the walls, designed to relieve the chamber of the immense heat generated by the plant's inner workings. All of those had been covered in what appeared to be a thick resin, slightly opaque and hardened, making Ajax think of the same fluids that would leak from a man's nose when he came down with a cold. With the heat trapped, the chamber was stifling, made more so by the oppressive humidity and the stench of rotting organic material.

The marine's boots crunched across the deck and Ajax looked down to see that while the walls and vents might be covered in the heavy, organic resin, the floor of the chamber was thick with tiny bones. It took Ajax a moment to realize that they were marching across hundred, perhaps thousands, of fish skeletons. It was difficult to see the whole chamber by the light of their three pulse rifles, but the marine took note that on the far side of the chamber there was an open pool of water with safety railing surrounding it. He realized that it was how the maintenance crews in dive suits were able to move in and out of the water. The railing was wickedly bent in a few places, as if something far too large to fit had forced its way through.

A wet crunching sound came from the darkness ahead, and all three marines converged their mounted lights on the source of the noise.

Jorumgandr was there, its thick wet hide sparkling as the lights reflected off it. The marines were veterans of hundreds of battles, had faced death and resurrection many times, but nothing in their long war with the garm had prepared them for what they witnessed.

The marines paused, fingers on the trigger, so shocked were they by the sight of it.

Jormungandr used one of its tentacles to push the crushed body of a human in workman's coveralls into its mouth, having unhinged its already huge jaws to make room for the grisly meal. The great beast's belly was massively distended, straining against the sheer amount of meat that had been stuffed inside it. As the corpse was being pulled wetly into the creature's mouth, the entire beast's body shuddered with effort and a grinding sound filled the chamber. Just like down in the sea caves, Ajax witnessed the gills at the base of the beast's neck flutter and expel gallons of blood and tissue. So focused was the beast upon its bizarre task that it paid no mind to the intruders, nor did it apply any psychic pressure upon the mind of Ajax.

The marine decided it looked like a sort of alien wood chipper, and the hideous thought snapped him out of his temporary shock as much as the cries of surprise that came from Skald Omar and the marines who entered behind the vanguard.

Ajax bellowed a war cry and squeezed the trigger of his pulse rifle, sending several plasma bolts towards the alpha garm. Jormungandr was not so bloated that it could not anticipate the attack, and the creature managed to jerk out of the way. Two bolts went wide and tore into the resin covered metal wall, creating a shower of sparks, and melted organic material, though one bolt did rend a gaping hole in one of the creature's tentacles.

Mahora shouted as he and Rama lent their fire to their comrade, only now their moment of advantage was lost, and the deadly speed of the alpha garm was telling. The creature was just as adept at moving above the water as it was below, using its tentacles to pull itself into the darkness.

The marines fired, their muzzle flashes and mounted lights struggling to track the beast through the engineering section. Bolts from their pulse rifles chewed up the walls and equipment in the chamber as they blazed away at the creature. Jormungandr's body convulsed and a cloud of barbs shrieked out of the darkness to impale Skald Omar and the marine standing next to him.

The marine collapsed in a heap with several barbs through his chest and neck, while Omar staggered backwards with one deep in his thigh.

Mahora roared and rushed the beast, firing as he ran, in an attempt to drive it into the far corner of the room. Ajax turned from the fight to glance at Omar, who had dropped his pulse rifle and fallen to his knees, beginning to seize from the poison in the barbs. The skald's mounted light illuminated the wall next to the entry hatch, and Ajax saw two dozen severed hands that had apparently been nailed to the wall.

Before his mind could process the curious display of carnage, Jormungandr's psychic howl for aide thundered across his mind and put Ajax on his knees.

It took the marine several harrowing moments to gain control of himself with his breath, and when he looked up, ripper drones were already emerging from the dive pool on the other end of the chamber. A scream of pain snapped the marine's attention over to Mahora just in time to see the jarl hurled several meters through the air and slam into a bank of cogitator units with one arm missing.

Jorumgandr was a writing mass of teeth and tentacles as it plowed through another marine, knocking the man aside as if he weighed nothing. The beast was more concerned with escape it seemed, than violence, and Ajax could see multitudes of terrible wounds troubling the creature. In the tight confines of the chamber, at this close quarters range, the pulse rifles of the Einherjar were especially devastating, even against an alpha garm such as this.

Omar went into convulsions as the poison flooded his system, prompting Ajax to thumb his pulse rifle over to full-auto.

Jormungandr stuffed itself through the entry hatch and disappeared up the stairs while Ajax turned his weapon on the ripper drones coming out of the pool. There were two of them already through, and a third climbing up. The marine cut loose and emptied his magazine at them, shattering their bodies with super-heated rounds, rending several holes in the walls behind them.

The pulse rifle clicked empty and he discarded it, knowing he did not have the time to vent the head or reload. He snatched up Omar's pulse rifle and raised it to his shoulders to empty yet another magazine into the rippers that were already rising to replace their slain kin. The marine that had been knocked down by the tentacles had risen to a crouching position and appeared to be shaking off the heavy hit and preparing to fire on the rippers also.

The pool was a natural choke point. That was an advantage for the marines, although an entire swarm might be trying to come up through there. If they didn't keep pouring on the fire on it would only take a matter of moments for an entire ripper swarm to fill the chamber and be in a position to sweep up from below to attack the defenders of the plant above.

"Get that alpha, we'll hold the drones!" growled Mahora, who was back on his feet and bracing his pulse rifle against the cogitator bank so that he could take shots at the rippers who continued to attempt breaching the chamber through the pool.

Ajax dropped the overheated rifle and sprinted towards the door, followed by one of the marines from Gorgon Company, as the others lent their fire to Mahora's against the drones. Ajax pounded up the steps, taking them two at a time, doing his best not to slip in the wide streaks of blood and ichor that the wounded Jormungandr was leaving behind. He pulled his pistol from its holster and pointed it ahead of him just as they entered the small hub, and managed to get several shots off as he saw Jormungandr squeezing its bloated self through the hatch that lead to the common room.

The small rounds blew chunks of meat out of the beast. In response, it convulsed to spew another cloud of barbs at the oncoming Einherjar. Time slowed for Ajax as he saw death streaking towards him, with nowhere to hide and no chance to move, he expected to be filled like a pin cushion.

Just before the barbs hit their mark, the marine who had joined him slammed into Ajax from behind. Ajax had the wind knocked out of him as he was shoved out of the way. One barb still tore through the visor on his helmet and pierced his left eye. Ajax fell to the deck. The marine who'd just saved his life was pierced by half a dozen of the deadly projectiles, causing the dying man to fall backwards.

Ajax grabbed the barb protruding from his faceplate and yanked it free, then scrabbled madly to get his helmet off. He couldn't be sure how much poison he'd just been injected with, if any at all, but he had certainly lost the use of his eye.

As the other marine's corpse clattered down the stairwell Ajax was confounded by the man's sacrifice. Yet more marines who bought into the Grendel story, and saw the continued survival of Ajax as critical to the resolution of the day's fighting. He had yet to decide what he believed, and found himself at once emboldened and angered by the dead man's tragic heroics. If men were going to step up and willingly take one step closer to blackout so that he could keep fighting then he'd better make good.

Ajax launched himself to his feet and into the common room, a snarl building in the back of his throat as he ran. He saw Jormungandr pressing its bulk out of the common room and onto the stairwell, and Ajax knew that the alpha garm was moments away from escape. They had to know why it was so important that the beast consumed the snail creatures, and why it launched a suicide attack against the rig just so it could gorge itself on what appeared to be the bodies of the maintenance staffers.

The marine knew his sidearm wouldn't do much more than slow the beast down, so as he rushed through the common room he pulled one of the jet-assist harpoons off the wall. His aim would probably be off thanks to the loss of the eye, but he had to keep going, had to keep fighting any way he could. Already he could feel himself beginning to weaken, and it was clear that at least trace amounts of poison had entered his body, even if the toxin-filled barb had not been able to empty itself.

Ajax emerged from the common room and found himself bathed in the dying light of dusk. All around him, above and below, a mighty battle raged as the swarms hurled themselves at the beleaguered marine defenses.

With his good eye, he squinted as he scanned for Jormungandr, not used to being in a combat situation without the visual enhancement of his helmet's ocular assist. The smears of blood and ichor went up and he saw that Jormungandr had heaved itself over the railing and was dragging itself across a gangplank that extended over the desalination device.

"Alpha Target on the move! Right above the central intake!" shouted Ajax over the company channel, and as he ran he saw several riflemen defending lower gangplanks and platforms turn their attention upwards. The defenders were being sorely pressed on all sides, but if even one more pulse rifle joined the struggle that was one more chance to bring this beast to heel.

The marine pushed himself even more, running as fast as he could up the steps and then leaping over the railing and onto the gangplank. Jormungandr saw him and again called for aide, forcing Ajax to concentrate on his breathing just as much as he was on forward progress. As Ajax held onto the thin railing of the gangplank, he kept putting one foot in front of the other, knowing that if he was going to be effective with the harpoon he had to get closer. Ajax fired the rest of his pistol magazine at the creature, more to interrupt its call than to hurt it, but even the one shot that did connect further damaged the already seriously wounded beast. In seconds the psychic pressure eased, and Jormungandr returned its focus to escape.

Ajax cursed aloud as he saw several shriekers break off their assault and form into two flights of angry monsters. One of the flights headed straight for him while the other flew out of his immediate sight. Ajax knew that in moments he would be a puddle of gore, and he had to make his play. The marine began sprinting across the gangplank, heedless of the multitude of acidic rounds that impacted around him. At least he was a moving target.

Above him a chainfire opened up, and soon the bodies of shriekers cascaded downwards on all sides. Ahead he saw the second flight of shriekers focus their attention on the gangplank, and instantly dozens of caustic assaults melted through the thin metal of the gangplank.

As Ajax ran, he saw the gangplank buckle and then suddenly bend. He realized that they were far enough away from the stable moorings of the central compound that gravity had become the enemy. There was more gangplank on his end than on Jormungandr's, and when the last bar dissolved, it was his side that began to arc downwards.

Ahead, he could see Jormungandr slowly pulling itself up the side of a platform. Beyond that was open sea. If it reached the platform there was nothing to stop it escaping. No nets and no marines. The two men who had been stationed there were now heaps of torn meat surrounded by the corpses of the shriekers they'd been fighting.

Ajax roared with frustrated rage as he surged forward, knowing that he was in the process of falling to his death. It made little difference, he knew he was dying from the poison, but he had to try. The marine's boots stomped across the falling gangplank as he thumbed the activator on the jet-assist and raised the harpoon to shoulder level with his right arm.

His left eye already a blind ruin, there was no need to squint as he did his best to line up his throw. Ajax squeezed the release handle as he hurled the harpoon with all his might. The harpoon sailed through the air for a moment, propelled by the muscles of the marine who threw it, and it would have fallen short but for the power of the jet-assist.

The tiny fuel pod built into the haft ignited and sent the harpoon slicing through the air, driving it deep into Jormungandr's already ravaged body. The barbed point pushed through the beast's thick flesh and embedded itself in the metal of the platform, pinning the thrashing beast in place.

Ajax's leap carried him in a wide arc downwards and he crashed into one of the catch buckets attached to the feeder line of the central system. His armor thudded dully and the marine's body bounced off the machine and fell further down to sea level. The rush of water filled the marine's awareness, but then, just as he was fully submerged, he was catapulted back up to the surface with a splash by the safety netting that covered the base of the plant's operation. Designed to save the lives of workers who fell, today it had become a graveyard, as hundreds of bodies covered the nets, both marine and garm alike.

The poison was beginning to make Ajax's muscles seize up, and it was all he could do to keep breathing as he rolled onto his back. Above him, he watched with a sense of cruel satisfaction as bolts from chainfires and pulse rifles reduced Jormungandr to a bloody alien pulp.

As he watched the beast's body come apart, its bloated stomach was torn and emptied itself into open air. What rained down onto the nets appeared to be a staggering number of partially digested human bodies.

They began to splash down around Ajax, and as his body finally gave in to the poison, the last thing he saw was the half-dissolved face of one of the bodies from Jormungandr's belly.

It was a man, or at least it had been, but to the dying marine it seemed like there was something not right about him.

Something not altogether human.

A STORM WITHOUT END

Ajax rested his arm on the barrel of his pulse rifle, the weapon slung over his shoulder, and let the rain wash over him. It had been a long time, too long to recall clearly, since he had enjoyed a good rain storm.

The forest moon of Khal was a place still untouched by the polluted cities of humanity, and when the rain fell it was free of toxins and sweet on the tongue. It was the little things like that which Ajax realized he'd grown accustomed to living without. The marines existed on packaged food and recycled water, with the occasional nutritional cocktail fed intravenously if their vitals were not in peak condition.

The worlds upon which the Einherjar trod were always war zones, from the shattered cities of Verdun 12 to the toxic swamps on Himar. The marine found himself oddly thankful that Task Force Grendel's mission had led them to a still pristine environment.

There was industry here, of course, but it was highly regulated and of minimum impact. Several ink-rock deposits had been discovered deep in the moon's core, and a single drilling compound had been sanctioned to extract. The rest of the moon was something of a nature preserve, though Ajax suspected that it wasn't open to the public so much as it was reserved for the elite of human society.

Ajax stood on a hill that looked down into a small valley, where the rest of Hydra Company had rallied. Beyond the valley, over a series of rocky hills and forested ridges, lay the drilling compound. Communication had been lost with the compound for several days, and like Kai Prime, that radio silence combined with the attention of the Bloodhound, spurred command to order *Bright Lance* to make haste. Orbital recon had given the impression that the compound was deserted. All the equipment had been shut down and not a soul could be seen moving about the site.

"Gorgon in position," came a voice over the company channel, soon followed by "Manticore in position."

"Hydra Company in position," said Jarl Mahora, "Break into your fire teams and hold your ground till Cerberus comes online."

Ajax and Hydra Company had made planetfall first and moved quickly to secure their current position. Thus far, no sign of the garm had been found, though Ajax was positive that the steadily increasing psychic pressure was emanating from the compound. He stood on the hill next to Hart, the sniper turned skald having been attached to his former marine company along with Omar and several other operators.

The men stood silently, using the large trunk of a tree as partial cover, which allowed them to have a clear view of the valley below and forest ahead. The only problem was the rain, sweet as it was. Air support from the *Edda* would have been desirable, though the heavy rain would make it nearly impossible for the pilots to register a shrieker suicide attack in time to evade it.

The willingness of the garm to choke the machines of humanity with their own bodies had once again put the infantry units at the vanguard. After years of war, Ajax was perfectly used to the vicious ground fighting without much in the way of air support. Artillery would do them little good here, given the thick canopy. Several tanks from Armor One had been assigned to Task Force Grendel, they lay idle, in wait for a battlefield that suited them. With the thick foliage, dense canopy, and a wilderness unspoiled by roads, it was upon the shoulders of the infantry that this battle would fall.

After Kai Prime, Ajax had no idea what to expect out of the garm this time. He had given a detailed report of what he'd witnessed in the sea caves, and his report raised more questions than it answered.

Thanks to Jormungandr, the snail creatures were pulped beyond recognition, and so Idris and his team had precious little to work with. Thus far they had no findings to report, and it was the same with the glowing green fluid, the only conclusion being a confirmation that whatever Jormungandr had done with its gills had made the fluid inert.

It was filled with cells and tightly packed DNA, but all so degraded that nothing could be gained from its study.

The bodies that had been ripped from the belly of Jormungandr were coated in a fluid that continued to break them down even after they had been freed from the confines of its digestive system. By the time marines could get down to the safety nets and recover the torc from Ajax's corpse, the marine's armored body was awash in a thick soup of digested meat. The fluid had begun to eat away at his combat armor. Had he remained suspended in it much longer his torc might have been damaged.

Ajax had made it clear to any who would listen that the bodies weren't completely human, but with no bodies to check, it was impossible to know for sure. He was already dying from the poison, and the other remains were badly decomposed, but the marine could not shake the certainty that they had been tampered with somehow, by the garm.

"You're thinking of those men back on Kai Prime, yes?" asked Hart, his voice cutting through the rain and snapping Ajax back to attention, the marine having drifted into his thoughts.

"Aye. One of them landed right next to me, and I know it could have just been damaged," grumbled Ajax, "But I'm sure it was more than that."

"Most are inclined to believe you, Ajax," said Hart, "Even without proof, your word counts for a great deal these days. Some say you are Beowulf incarnate, if the talk has any truth to it."

"Hindsight is always keen, it seems easier to put meaning on things that have already happened than it is to predict what will come," stated Ajax as he cast his gaze across the valley, which was nearly obscured by the falling rain. "Skald Omar insists that there are at least three alpha garm incursions to be rooted out, we are here for the second. He is trying to look ahead with his stories."

"The god, Loki, had three sons from the womb of the giantess, Angrboda," spoke Hart as he flipped open the cap that covered his scope and leaned in to peer through it. "We find one in the sea and call it Jormungandr, now we hunt Fenrir in dark forests. I have to wonder if we would face such horrors had we not named them so."

"What about the double-blind effect?" asked Ajax from his position just below the sniper. "I pinged on Kai Prime before anyone told us the story, or at least told me, of the serpent, Jormungandr."

"Ah yes, but once the beast was so named, did you not slay it in a manner befitting legend?" argued Hart with a bemused tone as he continued to look down his scope, the heavy rain making it difficult to see much, even with the sight assist features of his helmet. "We have pulse rifles, chainfires, even grenade launchers, and yet you strike the killing blow with what was essentially a spear. You accomplished this feat with the use of but a single eye."

"Odin, the one-eyed god with the enchanted spear," breathed Ajax, and he looked away from the sniper and down into the forest just below the hilltop upon which they were positioned, his eyes coming to rest on Hydra Company as the marine force awaited the coming conflict. "The similarities are impressive, and yet in the sagas, it was Thor and his hammer who slew Jormungandr. It's like the pieces of the sagas are all there, but we're putting them together differently in the living of it. I don't see how Omar can think anything can be predicted, the meaning of it all only makes sense looking backwards."

"It will drive you mad if you dwell on it too much, Ajax," said Hart before shifting his stance slightly so that he could rest more of his body against the trunk of the massive tree behind which the men had taken cover. "Skald Thatcher died attempting to cast himself as Beowulf instead of focusing on the approach that made the most tactical sense. Besting Grendel in single combat was a fool's errand, had he waited for the rest of us, perhaps he would yet live."

"The sagas seem to be an accurate road map, so far," observed Ajax, "At least by strokes broad enough to yield some measure of victory. Even Jarl Mahora seems to be taking the narrative more seriously."

"As am I, brother, your defeat of Jormungandr, and the manner of it, certainly adds to the mounting evidence from Heorot. Though you make an excellent point, all the pieces seem to be here, and that is of note, and yet events unfold as they do and it is only afterwards that we see the whole of it. Thor may have slain the serpent in legend, yet it is undeniable that you filled the role of Odin in that moment," replied Hart as he flipped down the cap and relaxed his grip on the rifle so that he could turn and face Ajax. "Perhaps there is something deeper at work here, a sort of archetypal momentum to our journey. My point is that we should be using the narrative as a supplement to sound military strategy. Thus far, Skald Wallace seems to be of the same temperament, despite how loudly Skald Omar may proselytize."

Ajax was silent, and found himself looking back down at Hydra Company as they began forming into small attack squads. Omar had, indeed, become much more vocal about the sagas after the events on Kai Prime. Ajax could not blame him, as it was undeniably serendipitous that Ajax should lose an eye and then slay the beast with the harpoon, even if those events were at odds with the exact details of the sagas. It was a living remix of the struggle between the mythic Jormungandr and the gods, down to Ajax killing the garm with a spear and then succumbing to the beast's poison. The marine could not deny that it was a rather powerful example of life syncing up with story, and taken alone, it could be considered coincidence, though when combined with the events on Heorot, it was downright chilling.

An increasing number of the Einherjar, from the rank and file grunts, to the special forces operators, to the officers in command, were open supporters of the sagas. In many ways, Ajax felt that the disjointed unfolding of events was the only thing preventing the All-Father's army from looking to the sagas as a core battle script instead of a curious supplemental advantage. It wasn't as though Ajax could have fought Jormungandr by himself, it still took legions of marines, air support, and sound military stratagems to carry the day.

"The men are looking for change," said Hart suddenly, "Deep down, we all know that if the war continues as it has, this grinding stalemate will see us all black out eventually and humanity annihilated."

"What about the new marine companies coming out of Bifrost?" asked Ajax, curious as to his comrade's nihilistic sentiment. "They'll be blooded veterans soon enough."

"Men do not volunteer so readily as they once did now that the threat of the garm is fully engaged. That urgency has dimmed somewhat for a civilization so far removed from our war. Especially considering how few arise with their minds intact from that first death and rebirth, as we were not ever meant to persist in this way. That being said, yes, there may be new companies founded on Bifrost, and perhaps they will be enough to maintain the stalemate," Hart shrugged. "The veterans, which are most of us, crave a war that can be won. That, more than any empirical evidence in support, is what brings warriors into the fold with the likes of Omar."

"Command didn't even hesitate to mobilize our forces when I let it be known that this forest moon throbbed in my psyche," said Ajax, at once encouraged by the faith that everyone showed in his abilities and filled with dread as to the level of responsibility that put squarely on his shoulders.

"The more victorious we are, the more fanatical we may become, and fanaticism breeds inflexibility," said Hart, more to himself than Ajax. The rain fall began to ease and he looked through his scope once more, this time with much less interference. "If you believed as hard as the others, you might have overlooked the harpoon in search of a hammer, and Jormungandr might have escaped. It is better that you are open minded, yet unconvinced."

They were dancing around the grisly spectacle of the severed hands that had been nailed to the interior wall of the engine section. It was a behavior undocumented in all the years of conflict against the garm, and the sight of it haunted him still. For what purpose would the garm do such a thing? They had never displayed an inclination towards decoration, or trophy taking, and even advanced organisms like Grendel and Jormungandr had focused on combat and recon. Psychological warfare was not something the garm conducted, at least not on a conscious level. The Hive Mind certainly engaged on a universe-wide psychic level, but even that did not have the sort of artful malice inherent in the atrocity.

Skald Omar had insisted during the debriefing that the hands and the way they were nailed to the wall in a large circle pointed to one of the Norse stories. In that tale, the trickster god Loki's misdeeds resulted in the sun god, Tyr, losing his hand, swallowed up by the beast Fenrir.

The skald was immediately shut down by Wallace before he could say more, and the discussion was tabled. Ajax could tell that the skalds were keeping something from the marines, and so could Jarl Mahora. The hardened veteran had chosen to let it go, insisting later to Ajax that they let the skalds keep their secrets, marines had better things to do.

Ajax dared not ask Hart, for even if the sniper knew something about the hands and their significance, the marine knew that the sniper would keep his silence. Their friendship was an awkward one, but based on mutual respect and years of fighting side by side, and Ajax did not care to upset that balance. Marines had better things to do than worry about what schemes the skalds were up to.

"Cerberus in position," came through the channel, and Ajax knew it was time for action.

The marine touched his fingers to his temple to give Hart a farewell salute, and then turned to make his way down the hill to join his fire team, his boots sinking into the loamy soil and crunching through the layer of pine needles that rested on top.

His comrades waited for him, men whose own reputations were beginning to take shape simply by their close association with him. Yao had swapped out his rifle for a grenade launcher, having been determined by the jarl to be the best suited replacement for Boone. Rama, Sharif, Ford, and Silas all stood by the freshly minted grenadier and shouldered their rifles as Ajax approached.

"Fire teams, fall in," growled Jarl Mahora over the company channel, "This will be just like the island, boys. We hit the objective from all sides, divide the swarms, and secure the compound building by building. There were two hundred and eighty people living and working here, and while I'm sure they ended up meat for the hive, let's hope there's somebody left to save this time. Move out!"

A PLACE AMONG THE PINES

Ajax was thankful for the steady downpour, as it masked the sound of so many marines moving through the forest. There was still plenty of natural light; by local time it was early morning, which meant they had plenty of time to get this mission done before nightfall, or at least they hoped. They did their best to pick their way through the dense trees, though the occasional snapping twig or sucking mud hole was unavoidable.

The Einherjar were trained soldiers to be sure, but moving through terrain and being on the offense was not a tactic generally employed by the marines. Thanks to the subtle and oppressive psychic pressure of the Hive Mind and the raw technical and tactical reality of fighting the garm swarms, the marines were far more used to defensive combat maneuvering. While they had all fought many times defending trenches and re-taking ditches that had been overrun, assaulting an objective at the outset of an engagement was still something they were getting used to.

The island assault on Kai Prime had shown them that Einherjar forces were indeed capable of going on the attack and actually winning. Now the warriors carried on with a sense of heightened purpose, eager to prove to themselves and the garm that marines could take a proactive stance. No longer could the garm rest comfortably in the knowledge that it was they who determined the particulars of battle.

Ajax found himself snarling quietly as he moved through the underbrush towards the compound, it was good to be the aggressor.

Ajax halted his advance just behind the treeline near the compound, recalling from the orbital photos that there was roughly a ten-meter perimeter around the compound that had been carved out of the forest. The crew of the facility maintained the perimeter, cutting back against the ever-encroaching forest that sought to re-take the ground seized by human ingenuity. The marine looked to his left and saw Hart using climbing spikes affixed to his wrists and boots to ascend one of the trees on the edge of the line.

The sniper gazed through his rifle scope for a few moments and then signaled the all clear down to the marines below. Ajax nodded and hefted his pulse rifle. The marine stepped out of the treeline and stalked double time across the open ground. No attacks came, and in moments Ajax and his fire team reached the cover provided by the elevated walkway that encircled the compound.

There were sizeable land predators indigenous to the forest moon, beasts similar to the wolves of ancient Earth, that incentivized the colonists to build the platform an extra meter off the ground. Ajax stood to his full height and grabbed the railing so that he could heft himself onto the platform, climbing the railing like a ladder before casting himself over the top.

It did not take long for the other fire teams to begin pouring over the railing and Ajax had his rifle up and started moving deeper into the compound.

It was a pre-fabricated facility, one of the newer models used by human colonists in the years just before the garm invasion. It could be dropped in a single massive cargo pod and then workers could un-pack and erect it within a matter of days. It reminded Ajax of the mobile fortress they'd deployed in the last days on Heorot, and the memory gave him a shudder.

Since its construction, the locals had made a number of modifications. Ajax saw several add-on habitation buildings made from converted cargo containers, in addition to the massive drill rig that jutted up from the center of the compound. The marine passed by a lift-gate set into the edge of the platform, which would allow for colonists to explore the rugged terrain, mostly astride the small ATVs that were so common among colonists that they were a symbol of the lifestyle itself.

The buildings were laid out in a simple grid, which made for easy navigation, though in a combat scenario it put the marines in a position of having to treat each intersection as a potentially hostile hard point. All those right angles made for excellent ambush points, and Ajax found himself thankful, for once, that they were facing alien creatures who did not fight like men.

Garm had little use for traditional urban warfare, preferring to either charge recklessly into the fray or swoop down upon the enemy and rely on the shock of their savagery and numbers to carry the day.

Ajax took note of several smears of blood across the decking and on the door of a building as the team entered the compound. Ajax pulled security with Silas as Ford and Rama entered the squat building.

"Are you seeing this?" asked Rama, his voice shaking with something close to fear as the other marines entered the building behind him.

It had been a supply shed, positioned near the lift-gate for easy access. There were several ATVs parked in the main area, and shelf upon shelf of tools, supplies, and raw materials that indicated that this was a maintenance building.

Ajax activated his mounted light to cut through the shadows and swept his gaze through the room illuminating the two bodies. One male and one female, who had died horribly.

"They look to have been tortured, don't they?" asked Ford as he knelt down next to the woman.

Ajax saw that while they had been finished off with extreme blunt trauma to the head, they did appear to have been mutilated prior to being slain.

"Garm don't do this," muttered Rama, shaking his head and backing away from the corpses.

All of them were feeling sick, and Ajax knew exactly why. Each of them had seen terrible violence in their long war with the garm, and none of them were a stranger to the torn bodies of humans. However, the garm were not sadists, simply nightmarishly efficient killing and eating machines.

There was a deliberate malice to this that none of them had experienced thus far, and for the first time in their long careers as soldiers they were unsure of their path forward.

"Yao, call it in," ordered Sharif suddenly, the marine stepped forward and firmly herded his men, including Ajax, out of the building. "We stay on mission. Our job is to find the garm and kick ass. Leave this for the skalds."

"We aren't the only ones to find this sort of thing," said Yao, a haunted edge to his voice after reporting their findings, his ear filled with chatter of similar grisly discoveries.

"But who would do this and why?" protested Rama, allowing himself to be shepherded away from the grisly scene, "People don't fight people anymore."

"Lock it up, Rama," said Sharif, "Ajax, take point."

The marines returned to the wet outdoors, and continued deeper into the compound.

The rain was relentless and Ajax could see the complex gutter system the riggers had put in place to handle the runoff. It was as he cautiously stepped forward to look more closely at the drainage system that he caught the shimmer of movement on the low roof adjacent. His instincts screamed at him to retreat into cover, but Silas was already in position behind him.

"*Shooter high and right!*" shouted Ajax as he hurled himself across the open intersection, knowing that if there were more shooters he'd just run into their sights while avoiding the former.

Silas was able to pull back behind the wall just as a series of shots rang out, the high-pitched crack of conventional firepower ringing out against the morning rainstorm. Bullets ripped through the cheap metal of the decking and the wall near Silas, though the marine's combat armor easily deflected the shrapnel.

Ajax hugged the wall and began moving down the intersection towards the shooter, staying just out of sight thanks to the oversized gutters installed on the edges of each building.

The shooter kept up a sporadic, but punishing rate of fire which kept the rest of the team behind cover, though Ajax had the distinct impression that this was not sustained suppressive fire. It lacked the methodical pacing that a trained soldier would display, making Ajax think that it was more likely a civilian with a high capacity rifle.

Colonists were known to bear arms, as was their right, especially when they were settling a rugged wilderness such as this. However, why they would shoot at the marines who'd come to rescue them was indeed a mystery.

More shots echoed through the downpour and the company channel erupted with radio chatter. Apparently, there were hostiles all over the compound, and once fire teams had begun to penetrate the facility an opposing force was lashing out. Everyone, including Ajax, was temporarily at a loss about who they might be fighting or why. While they had been at war with the garm for years, not a single marine among them had fought a human being. There were some, like Jarl Mahora, who had been professional soldiers during the intercene corporate wars that were interrupted by the garm invasion, though they were in the extreme minority.

While Ajax moved to position himself underneath the shooter's position, his actions were more based on instinct, and he was hesitant to raise his rifle once he was there.

Was humanity not aligned as a single force against the garm? How could anyone think to stand against the Einherjar? Every man, woman, and child recognized the armor and weapons of these legendary warriors. Why attack the very soldiers dedicated to your protection?

The sharp cracks of the rifle were joined by the voices of other conventional weapons throughout the compound, though the other marines were just as confused and hesitant as Ajax. They weren't trained to fight people, and the killing of a human being was so outside the paradigm of the garm fighters that not a man among them had returned fire. Casualty reports began to ring out, and it was clear that they faced a sizable enemy force.

"*Defend yourselves, marines!*" bellowed Jarl Mahora over the company channel, his voice and command code silencing the multitudes of reports from other beleaguered fire teams. "Garm or not, they've stepped up, so put 'em down!"

Ajax sucked in his breath and raised his pulse rifle. He had followed the shooting to just underneath the enemy, and sure enough as another shot rang out, a spent shell rolled off the roof and clattered into the gutter. The marine pushed off the wall and spun around, aiming his rifle upwards as he did so. The shooter filled the marine's iron sights, and Ajax could not help hesitating.

The man was dressed in the filthy coveralls of a rig staffer, complete with ink-rock stains on his outfit, but it was his face and hands that gave the marine pause.

The man was smiling, not the sort made of mirth, but the wicked grin borne of madness. His eyes were wide open, lips pulled back to reveal bloodstained teeth, and it appeared that he had been engaged in violence based on the wounds Ajax could see. The shooter didn't notice him at first, but then those wide, mad eyes glance downwards and the rifle began to move in the marine's direction.

"*Meat!*" howled the man, and the familiar battle cry snapped Ajax out of his paralysis.

The marine squeezed the trigger and sent a bolt through the man's face. As the round crushed his nose, the heat from it expanded outwards to obliterate the skull. The headless corpse collapsed in a heap and the dead hands dropped the rifle. Ajax took a second breath and then keyed his mic.

"*They're ragmen! Repeat, ragmen!*" shouted Ajax as Silas moved from cover and the rest of the fire team filled the intersection.

"Wipe them out!" responded Mahora, "Watch for ridgebacks on the perimeter. Fire teams not already engaged, set up defensive positions on the platform."

Ajax started marching forward, sweeping his pulse rifle up to check the rooftops and side to side to cover the streets as he moved. He could feel the garm presence strongly, and was drawn towards the center of the facility.

So powerful was the pull that he had to center his breathing just to focus on the threat at hand. His discipline paid off, and he was poised for action when a ragman leapt out of a doorway and began firing wildly at the marines.

Ajax filled his iron sights with the ragman and put two bolts through the hostile's chest. The man's torso exploded outwards, sending smoking flesh in all directions, and where the man fell a fine red mist hung in the air just inside the door and away from the rain.

More shooting reverberated off the metal surfaces and Ajax scrambled for cover behind a stack of cargo containers, held in a tight stack by netting. Bullets threw sparks against the rain as several ragmen charged into what Ajax realized was a small cargo plaza.

He looked to his side and saw Sharif taking cover behind a stationary crane, and took note that the crane must have been part of the original fabrication process, left to wait in case the platform was ever taken down.

Ajax shook his head, casting the image of the exploding man out of his mind. He'd put down many a garm in his day, and more than a few ragmen, but there was something horribly different about killing a colonist. The Einherjar were, for better or worse, used to killing their own when a marine became a ragman, but they were out of their element, fighting an offensive action against human opponents. There was something about fighting otherwise civilian combatants that took some effort to cope with.

More shots pinged off the cargo containers and brought Ajax back into the fight. However, the fire team was rising to the challenge. Ajax saw Rama and Silas assaulting one of the ragmen snipers while Ford laid down suppressing fire. A concussive explosion ripped through the plaza and sent the torn remains of another ragman sailing through the air, splattering across the deck near Ajax's position.

"Yao took to the grenade launcher nice and quick, didn't he?" joked Rama over the team channel, his voice bookended by roars of his pulse rifle, ending the life of the ragman sniper.

"Boone wouldn't be impressed," answered Yao, "I don't think that's in his DNA."

Ajax laughed despite himself. It wasn't the best set of jokes in the world, but it was something he could hold onto. It was enough.

The marine launched himself from behind the crates and strafed the position of a ragman who had been pelting Sharif and the crane with clouds of buckshot. The first two bolts went wide, but the third vaporized the ragman's right arm and enough of his side that Ajax could see the pink of lungs and the white of ribcage. Any other human being, even an Einherjar marine, would have gone down after that kind of damage, but not the garm-spoor infected ragmen.

"*Meat*!" howled the ragman as he charged Ajax, seemingly intent on tearing the marine apart with his bare hands.

Ajax fired from the hip and his shot blew the ragman into pieces. The marine then swept his rifle around and saw that the fire team was forming up on his position. There were firefights all across the compound, but they'd earned themselves a brief reprieve.

"The garm are in the rig," said Ajax flatly, meeting the eyes of his fire team as they looked at him expectantly.

"Then let's drop every ragman from here to there," answered Sharif as he tucked his rifle stock into his shoulder and proceeded forward.

WOLVES

Rama staggered backwards as a ragman burst out of a shipping container, blazing away with a shotgun as he rushed the marine. The first blast was at a sufficient distance to spread the deadly shot, and though a cloud of projectiles hit the marine, they were mostly stopped by his armor. It was the second shot that pushed the marine back and damaged his pulse rifle, the third cracked the armor protecting his chest, and the fourth finally shredded his torso with buckshot.

A bolt from Ajax struck the ragman and sent his body spiraling to the ground in a super-heated storm of viscera. The marine had been providing bracketing fire for Sharif so that the man could flank and eliminate another ragman. His tenth consecutive round fired, Ajax raised the barrel of his rifle and Ajax ducked back into cover behind a small forklift as he vented the heat of his pulse rifle.

While these ragmen were certainly different from those he had experienced in the past, they died the same, which was at least something.

They had no sense of strategy or unit cohesion, which was typical, though they were able to perform some degree of critical thinking, which was profoundly disturbing. The fact that they were actually *using* their weapons instead of simply resorting to close quarters attacks had made progress through the compound slow going.

As he and the fire team fought their way deeper into the compound they were soon joined by other teams from Hydra as the company swept across their quadrants.

The psychic pressure was growing, and Ajax felt the alpha garm cry out for aide. Like Jormungandr's, it was a psychic keening that very nearly put Ajax on his back. The marines were still at least one block away from the rig, having marched over the bodies of dozens of ragmen, though not a single ridgeback had been spotted.

"Ajax, you okay?" asked Ford as he crouched down next to the marine.

"The alpha garm is definitely in the rig, I just felt it call for a swarm," muttered Ajax as he struggled to his feet, his rifle again at the ready.

Ajax toggled his comms over to the command channel as more waves of psychic pressure crashed against him. He paused for a moment when he realized that the waves were coming from the swarm that was responding. Two distinct psychic impressions occupied his mind, and Ajax understood that his ability to filter and control what he was sensing had become more potent. With use comes mastery, he thought to himself grimly before opening the channel.

"Jarl Mahora, the alpha garm is here. I feel it in the rig," announced Ajax, "But that's not all. It called for swarms and swarms answered."

"Roger, Ajax, I'm getting updates from command. They're registering heat sources that weren't there before, and closing in on us from all sides," acknowledged Mahora,

"Looks like the bastards buried themselves to avoid orbital detection," snarled Mahora before announcing, "We've got swarms on the surround! Fire teams not presently engaged get into position on the compound walls and prepare to repel attackers. Get these ragmen finished, marines!"

"Ajax, I am closing on the rig," chimed Skald Omar. "We will meet you in the middle."

Ford and Ajax leapt out from behind cover and rushed to join Sharif and Silas, who had taken up position at the mouth of an alleyway that lead out into the rig plaza. Above them they heard the signature report of Hart's sniper rifle. A welcome sound, considering that they could already hear the rumble of garm swarms, the pounding of their feet upon the earth reverberating through the cheap metal of the compound decking.

"Rippers and gorehounds on the approach," reported Hart over the command channel, punctuating his statement by firing a heavy round.

"No shriekers, no ridgebacks, no UltraGarm. This swarm is even less versatile than the last, they have the numbers, though I'm not seeing any of the environmental adaptations as reflected in Jormungandr's brood."

"Our enemy had less time to prepare before our arrival," responded Omar as he and two skalds appeared on the other side of the plaza and signaled to Ajax, gesturing with his hands at a large rollup docking bay and the access door adjacent. "Jormungandr likely had months to develop its brood, while Fenrir, whatever it reveals itself to be, has had mere weeks. Our bloodhound is running them to ground. Ready marines?"

"Overwatch, ready," stated Hart.

"Assault, ready," said Ajax.

"Go!" shouted Omar.

At Omar's signal the marines sprinted across the open ground, keenly aware that they would be easy targets for any ragmen still active in the area, made only marginally less so by their speed.

As the marines pounded over the deck, they heard the boom of the high caliber sniper rifle and the body of a ragman came crashing down onto the metal. A second shot rang out, and this time Ajax saw that Hart was hitting men who had emerged from the thick forest of scaffolding higher up on the rig. A third man fell to Hart's rifle, and then the marines were safe under the metal awning just beneath the docking bay.

One more shot rang out, and a body splattered onto the deck just behind the marines.

"Scaffolding clear," reported Hart. "Repositioning to outer perimeter defense, maybe I can get the WarGarm before it reaches the walls."

"Good hunting," responded Omar, who then produced a telescoping rod that extended out to six inches and became instantly white hot.

Skald Omar pushed the rod into the lock on the door and in seconds the entire mechanism was slagged. The skald returned the tool to his belt and hefted his rifle.

"Now for the wolf, my brothers," he said with a smile. He shouldered the door open and rushed into the room with his rifle raised, followed by the two skalds and then the marine fire team.

The Einherjar swept into the rig interior, a wall of pulse rifles at the ready and were immediately met with a grisly sight indeed. While many dozens of armed ragmen had offered stiff resistance to the marine advance, it became clear where the rest of the facility's residents had ended up.

Ajax was reminded of the two victims he'd seen upon first entering the compound, only here there had to be the bodies of at least half the population. It appeared that most of them were laid out in piles, and after a few moments the men noticed that they were organized by gender.

It was difficult to tell the exact number, partly due to the limited visibility inside the rig, as only the body lights and mounted lights of the marines gave any illumination.

They dared not fire any flares for fear that the rig had fallen into disrepair. One spark upon a single crude spill could set off a chain reaction that would turn the rig into an explosive column of fire.

"Ragmen don't have this level of intellect," said Sharif with a tone of disbelief in his voice.

"They aren't supposed to use guns, either," observed one of the skalds as the formation moved deeper into the rig, passing by the piles as they went.

"Could it be that they were controlled somehow?" asked Silas as he looked closer, witnessing what had to be evidence of both cannibalism and torture. "The way the WarGarm direct the swarm?"

"Considering the bio-tech that was being utilized by Grendel upon its victims, to transmit psychic signals much like what our man, Ajax, is able to sense, I would venture a guess that it's likely what we are witnessing," breathed Skald Omar as he moved his light over a pile of bodies and then slowly up a nearby wall. "Having ragmen perform such foul deeds, execute basic instructions, use firearms, it all points to another kind of weapons test. One of control and influence. There is a plan unfolding before us."

The skald's light moved along the wall to illuminate dozens of hands that had been affixed to the wall with what appeared to be an industrial boltgun. They moved in patterns that made Ajax's mind reel, as if the alternating spirals and lines of the pattern were emanating a sort of psychic vibration. Skald Omar's eyes were wide as he took in the sight of it.

"And when the gods grew too bold, the great wolf Fenrir snapped his jaws to swallow the hand of Tyr," spoke Omar, loud enough for them all to hear, but seemingly to himself.

"Skald, look!" cried Ford.

The assembled warriors followed the beam of light from his rifle to see a small pool in which one of the sizeable snail-like garm was bathed in a slimy, clear fluid.

The marines added their lights to his and as they did so, a low growl began to build in the room.

Ajax felt the psychic pressure increase rapidly. He *knew* the alpha garm crouched above them in the darkness. He did not know with his conscious mind where the beast was, and yet his instincts screamed at him to act, so he did.

"Garm above!" shouted Ajax as he toggled his rifle to full-auto and sprayed the darkness up and ahead of him with bolt rounds.

His light moved across scaffolding, rig equipment, and several platforms, kicking up sparks and slag as the fusillade chewed through the metallic terrain. While his salvo might have been undisciplined, the alpha garm's terrible form was partially revealed in the sharp illumination of sparks and the sweeping of the rifle's mounted light.

It was menacingly huge, crouching upon a platform with mighty claws and bedecked in scything blades, and as it leapt out of the light, Ajax caught a glimpse of the telltale bio-weapon protruding from its back. It was as if the garm had found a way to cross-breed the UltraGarm with the ridgebacks to create a beast that had the features of both and a size somewhere in the middle.

The roar it made with its double-hinged jaws thundered through the rig interior, so loud that the audio-dampeners inside their helmets, which kept the marines protected from the report of their own weapons, were nearly overwhelmed.

Ajax squeezed the trigger again only to find that he'd overheated the rifle. He knelt to vent the heat, but he knew that it would be seized up for several critical moments. As one, the rest of the assembled warriors opened fire, filling the darkness of the rig interior with the strobe of seven mighty weapons spitting death. Fenrir was fast, much nimbler than its biological predecessors, and the Einherjar tore apart the rig as they chased it with punishing fire.

"Hold fast, brothers!" bellowed Jarl Mahora over the command channel, and Ajax realized that the swarm must have crossed into the clearing. "They die on the wall! No garm gets through today!"

Sharif screamed and Ajax looked up to see the marine shorn in two by the scything blades of the beast as it galloped past him.

He saw, in flashes of muzzle flare, that the withering fire of so many rifles had taken its toll on the beast. As it came around to fatally gore one of the skalds, its cloven hoof pulping Ford's right leg, Ajax knew it was going to take much more to put it down. He slung his rifle and slid his pistol from its holster, knowing that while the sidearm could do little to pierce the beast's thick hide, they would still hurt.

The beast suddenly halted and changed direction, swiftly plowing through Ford as the man attempted to get out of the way. Yao was somewhere behind Ajax, and the marine had apparently decided that killing the beast was worth the risk of turning the rig into an inferno.

Ajax heartily agreed with the sentiment, and he continued to pelt the beast with his pistol as the distinct sound of Yao's grenade launcher met his ears.

Fragmentation grenades, set with micro-timers to airburst, suddenly blossomed with fire and fury around Fenrir, and the beast howled in pain. More explosions rocked the rig interior and blasted great chunks of meat from the creature.

Silas was consumed in the blasts, his body punished by shrapnel and the concussive force from the grenades. Ajax looked behind him to see and hear Yao screaming, though Ajax could not tell if it was that he'd given into the black or that he'd slain a brother with friendly fire.

Ajax felt the monster crying out for its swarms, and felt the surge of the enemy press against the waves of death already being visited upon them. It haunted Ajax how he was able to feel not just the alpha garm, but now some abstract elements of the swarms of lesser garm organisms also.

Fenrir charged through the strobing light of muzzle flares and mounted lights towards the pool, and Ajax realized what it was about to do.

Fenrir scooped the garm snail-like creature from the pool and held it tightly in its multi-hinged jaws, though instead of immediately chomping it, the beast turned and fled.

Without thought, Ajax sprinted after the monster and saw that it was rushing down the sloped loading dock towards the roll up metal bay door. The door had been shredded by shrapnel from Yao's grenades, but even moderately intact he knew that the thing would go through it like paper.

The marine pumped his legs and pushed himself as fast as he could go, thinking less about what he was going to do when he reached the beast, and more about simply catching up to it.

Pulse rifles barked behind him and he saw Fenrir stumble as multiple bolts ruined one of its hind legs. The opportunity presented itself and without thinking, Ajax leapt upon Fenrir's back and plunged his trench spike into the meat between the creature's massive shoulders.

Fenrir roared in frustration and agony, but managed to regain its footing and tear through the bay door. Ajax's combat armor kept him from being sliced apart by the ragged edges of the cheap metal, but it was all he could do to hold on as the creature sprinted across the rig plaza. The beast's jaws snapped and Ajax heard the sound of the snail's body being pulped and cursed. All of this death and the alpha garm still got what must be the critical component of their radical evolution.

Angered by what felt like the futility of it, tired of being one step behind, Ajax began firing with his pistol. His rounds didn't do much, but fired right into the thing's body it they certainly got the monster's attention. The beast roared and started slamming its side into buildings and shipping containers as it ran in an attempt to knock Ajax away. He held fast, though only barely.

"Alpha garm approaching from the rear!" shouted Hart over the command channel. Ajax heard the report of his rifle just as the behemoth shuddered from the impact of a massive sniper round.

Ahead, Ajax could see the wall of the compound. Behind the thin barriers of wire and sheet metal the marines of Hydra Company held their ground against swarms of gorehounds and ripper drones. These weren't ideal defenses, though the open ground had made for an excellent killing field. Since the brood had only weeks to grow, the swarms were not very large compared to what the marines were used to fighting. Without air support from shriekers or artillery from the ridgebacks, it was all the ripper drones and gorehounds could do to take out what few marines they could before being mercilessly gunned down.

Fenrir was weakening, Ajax was sure, but its size and momentum would be enough to carry it through the barricades. Several marines attempted to flank it, and though they hit it with a few shots, Fenrir was deadly with its bio-weapons, and the beast left corpses in its wake, cleaved and bloody.

Ajax lost his grip and fell, smashing against the wall of a shipping container just before the creature reached the marine perimeter.

He rolled onto his stomach, looking up just in time to see Jarl Mahora appear from the ranks of marines who were focused on battling the swarm. The hardened veteran walked towards the charging beast, revealing that he had a pulse rifle in each hand. Majora pulled the rifles tight into the crooks of his elbows and squeezed the triggers.

The rifles were on full-auto, and as Fenrir bore down on him, Mahora unleashed a hurricane of bolts. The alpha garm's body was reduced to a hulk of burning meat, though its momentum carried it right over Mahora. The veteran's body was transfixed by one of the bio-blades, but even as he was dying, the man spewed curses and blood on his enemy, drawing his pistol and firing until finally he collapsed.

Ajax pushed himself to his feet and unslung his own pulse rifle. He was limping from what he assumed was a broken leg, his breath was short and painful enough to indicate many broken ribs and he could only hold the rifle with his right hand as the left was broken. He might not be able to do much, but after what he'd just witnessed, he knew that it was the duty of the Einherjar to press on.

Soon his iron sights were filled with the bodies of ripper drones, and though they might have failed to discover whatever it was the garm were up to on Khal, they'd certainly wipe them off the face of the forest moon.

SHAPESHIFTERS WALK ALONE

Loki breathed deep and slow, allowing the fetid air of the subterranean lair to fill his multi-chambered lungs. Though filtered through several membranes that had developed in his nose and mouth, the stench of offal and refuse was thick in his awareness. He found that the smell no longer offended him, so fascinated was he by the degree to which he could perceive the delicate minutiae of sensory input he was now capable of processing. His clawed fingers clicked against his knees as he remained in his full lotus position, a meditative posture that had always served him well in his former life as Skald Thatcher.

Just as he thought of himself as someone different, his body had evolved to reflect that inner change in the physical realm. His stocky frame had spent months changing since his immersion in the pool. Without his meditations, the process would have been unbearably painful.

The green fluid secreted by the creatures he'd taken to calling garm whelks, as they reminded him of the lightning whelk snails on Tarsis Prime, had ignited a radical change in him. Certainly, the Usurper had influenced his awareness, and he understood that the fluid was a sort of mutagenic cocktail that directly affected the DNA of anything it came in contact with. At the will of the hive mind this muta-gene could make and unmake bio-systems.

It was a messy process, one filled with suffering and dead ends as much as it was an evolutionary success. It was less like science and more of a wild expression of nature.

Loki stretched his elongated arms wide and flexed his clawed hands. The trial and error of a millennia of adaptations, scaled to the individual level and guided by the hive mind. At least that was how it had started, in the seemingly distant days of Grendel, the first of the muta-garm and the catalyst for the awakening of the Usurper.

Loki had to concentrate on the names he'd chosen for the garm and the hive mind, as the psychic presence was slippery and cunning. Always, it sought to dominate him, even if they operated as allies of a kind. Unless, of course, thought Loki grimly, he was already the pawn of the swarm. He slowly extended his legs and stood to his tremendous new height. Always, he wondered if his decisions were his own or those of the Usurper, which had become an ever-present force in his mind, even if it seemed to lack much in the way of its former vitality.

The Alpha Hive Mind had continued its purge of the Usurper. Even during these short months, Loki became strongly convinced that the fledgling hive mind survived only thanks to the efforts of himself and the men of the *Angrboda*. Where the Usurper was hidden, Loki could not fathom, and he was beginning to suspect that whatever was left of the garm intellect and psychic presence was present now only in its children.

Jormungandr was dead, as was Fenrir, their broods shattered and run to ground. They had served their purpose, indeed, though he was beginning to understand that the garm were not without awareness of the loss of their swarms. He'd felt the shockwave of Jormungandr's death while still en route to the forest moon, and it was the explosive end of Fenrir that had sent him to his knees but yesterday.

Still, he felt the Usurper in the back of his mind, somewhere in the shadows, whispering to him of terrible things.

Loki was only vaguely humanoid now, more so without his armor, which he had taken to wearing less and less as he explored his vast new array of sensory capabilities. Balor had been sorely tested to modify the Einherjar armor to accommodate his master's rapidly evolving form, but had risen to the occasion. Balor was a master craftsman, one of the best in the All-Father's army before defecting alongside the others of Thatcher's veteran force.

Loki strode to the corner of his chosen chamber and began the lengthy process of donning his modified combat armor. There was a fight coming, he could feel the psychic shivers of Ajax projecting himself like a drag net across human space. Loki might have the discipline and control to mask his own presence, but Hel had reached maturity. She might be the greatest of the muta-garm spawn he'd rescued from the dying hive ship, but she was still a wild and alien thing. While Loki could intentionally reduce his own psychic emanations, a skill learned by skald training and perfected by his daily struggle for independence with the Usurper, Hel was incapable of such levels of thought and intent.

Grendel had been both a catalyst and an anomaly, Loki had come to believe, and none of the beasts since that nightmare creature had entered the world were its equal. Unless, of course, one counted Loki himself, who in his current form was something of a bastard child of Grendel and his human parents, as much as he was a product of the body forge now warped by the garm muta-gene. This was a thought that the former skald had considered several times.

Regardless, Hel was not yet ready to make her journey, and it would not take long for Ajax to ping on Hel's presence upon this urbanized world. It was possible that the dense population of Tankrid could obfuscate her presence from the Bloodhound for a time, the hero marine had proven himself adept at finding the children *Angrboda* left in its wake. Just as well, thought Loki as he slid his hand into the armored glove crafted to accommodate his clawed fingertips, it was time to face the Einherjar at long last.

Let them gaze upon the architect of doom, snarled Loki inside his mind, a sentiment shared by the presence of the Usurper the moment he expressed it. The former skald's shoulder pieces had been elongated to rise up to either side of his helmet, which allowed his now advanced hearing to not only pick up audio, but echo locate in the darkness of the Tankrid underworld. Loki's helmet now had seven ocular ports cannibalized from the spare marine helms in the Angrboda's equipment locker, one for each of the sensory organs that had sprouted from his face.

The hideous warrior leaned down and picked up a heavily modified firearm, which was now a combo weapon capable of toggling between the pulse rifle that served as its base and a conventional sub-machine gun. They fought men now, not just the garm, and a forward-thinking warrior carried weapons suited to his purpose. The torcs of his fallen comrades and those murdered in their escape from the Bifrost jingled upon Loki's chest, and he ran a sharp, armored finger over them. There would be more still, to hang upon him before this journey was ended.

As he checked the magazine of the rifle and re-inserted it, Unferth entered the chamber. Unferth, like the others, still maintained the bulk of his human traits, and it was only the small details that gave away the warrior's subtle adaptations. The skalds and other men who had survived the battle for the hive ship were as yet untouched by the muta-gene itself. Over time they had become deeply in thrall to Loki's psychic influence and delicately warped by Loki's spoor upon them, as the garm substance had only recently been perfected. It was a delicate process of determining the ideal form of the substance and the appropriate delivery system. Much had been learned by the trials and errors of those who had gone before. The broods of Jormungandr and Fenrir were sacrifices upon the altar, now it was time for his own brood to do the same.

"Tankrid deputies have begun probing the tunnels several districts over," reported Unferth, "According to our local sources the city powers occasionally conduct purges of the various undesirables that live here. It will not take them long to realize that there is nobody left to purge."

"The swarm needs a few more days to mature. If Hel feels threatened she will hatch them early, before their adaptations are fully developed, and we will have lost our chance to harvest the weapon," responded Loki as he made to leave the chamber alongside Unferth. "Have the men patrol the edge of our domain, if it looks like the deputies will cross into hive territory eliminate them. Stealth kills would be ideal. If we are lucky and it takes them another day or so to reach us, those deputies will be our field test before the Einherjar arrive. I can feel Ajax searching and have no doubt he will soon be at our door."

Unferth turned sharply at the door and went down a tunnel that led towards the central hub. The skalds were adept warriors, and Loki had perfect trust that they would do as asked.

Loki continued down the passage adjacent to his personal chamber, and soon the narrow tunnel widened, opening to a massive drainage exchange. Mucus had been used with great effect to create hardened resin barriers that directed the flow of sewage throughout the chamber in such a way as to allow the egg chamber to co-exist with a functioning sewage system. It would not do to have the local municipality noticing that their system was not functioning, and so long as it flowed, then none were the wiser as to the horrors being bred beneath the mega-city streets.

Loki walked into the chamber and leaned over one of the eggs. It was so very near hatching, and he could see where the hide of the shell was growing thin, a sure sign that the nightmare inside was nearly ready. The former skald then let his multiple eyes come to rest upon the resin breeding pool that Hel had created just to the side of the chamber. The stinking sluice of partially digested human corpses rippled as umbilical cords drew nutrients from the bottom of the pool and fed them to the clutch of slightly less developed eggs near the top of the stack.

Not all of them would be hatched and ready when the Einherjar came, thought Loki to himself with a surprising tinge of sadness, but with a hard fight between the marines and this chamber perhaps enough would be ready to make a difference.

There was a sudden psychic pressure that pushed down on Loki, and he looked up to see the eight-legged terror that was Hel slowly descending from the ceiling. He no longer controlled her, though honestly, he had begun to wonder if the influence he'd had over the likes of Jormungandr and Fenrir was him or just the Usurper using him like a puppet.

She must have sense his growing concern, for her stance was a defensive one, a subtle message that even he was less important than her clutch.

He reached out to her with his mind, and found Ajax already heavy upon her. The warriors of humanity were coming.

Time to put the final pieces into play.

UNDERWORLD

Deputy Springer did his best not to stare, though that was proving more difficult than he'd expected. When the leadership element of the Einherjar warriors had first entered the precinct he had stared then, too. What more could one expect of a man who was but a child when the extinction fleet first appeared on the fringes of human space?

He remembered the terror in his parent's voices when they told him of the wolves at the gate. His father was swept up by the planetary tithe, as Tankrid was not spared participation in the war effort. They were a working-class family, with no money to avoid the tithe, and so his father was pressed into service. Springer's father died, of course, like most of the millions of soldiers hurled into battle against the swarms in the early years of this terrible war.

When the Einherjar were created they seemed like gods striding across display screens large and small as the citizens of Tankrid, just like every other human city he assumed, marveled at the warrior's humanity had created to fight the alien menace. That was over a decade ago, and as not a soul on Tankrid had ever seen one in person, the might and glory of the Einherjar had faded.

It reminded him of something Deputy Stratton had told him once, when Springer was a rookie on his first purge, that humanity had forgotten the danger.

That was easy to do on Tankrid, thought Springer, as life in the mega-city was a busy one, indeed. If you were rich you had to hustle to stay that way, and if you were poor you had to struggle just to survive. This was a society in decline. Springer had come to agree with Stratton, and it was no wonder that the community officers of generations past had been replaced with militarized deputy forces.

Not that Deputy Springer felt all that militarized in the presence of these near mythic warriors from the frontlines. He was strapped into a mag-rail that was in the process of taking several companies of

Einherjar across the mega-city towards their destination. They were armored from head to toe and carried wicked looking rifles the likes of which Springer had only read about or seen in still life. Compared to these warriors, the dozen deputies under Springer's command seemed like glorified security guards, not hardened sewer cops, though each man among them had served his time in the underworld.

Their service record, and Springer's, was the reason the prescient had chosen them to accompany this Einherjar force. One hundred deputies from across Tankrid had been summoned at the behest of the man who sat across from Springer, one Skald Omar, operating with the full authority of something called Task Force Grendel. These were grim men indeed, and from what he gathered, listening to their small talk these warriors had been hunting a particularly difficult enemy force.

The thought that the garm had somehow broken through the Einherjar battle lines and infested Tankrid sent chills up Springer's spine, and he flexed his hands open and closed to give himself something to do with his excess nervous energy.

He noticed the man named Omar and a warrior sitting next to him with the name Ajax stenciled across his chest, both looking at him, though they at least did him the courtesy of not saying anything.

Everyone had been told, even if they'd forgotten, that facing the garm would do strange things to a man's mind. In fact there were rumors that the Hive Mind actually played psychic tricks on humanity in general, pushing civilization into a siege mentality. He didn't know much about that, but what he did know was that he was a solid sewer cop, even if that slang term was somewhat derogatory, as it applied to the men who policed all of the lower city levels, not just the stinking tunnels beneath the streets. Just one more way for the elites to lord over them he supposed, though, in that moment, he was just glad to have these strange warriors at his side.

He could not have imagined facing a garm infestation with just deputies. His father may have died for humanity, but Springer very much wished to survive for humanity. He did, after all, have a wife and a baby on the way. It seemed cruel that he be called to serve on such a mission considering his pending fatherhood, and yet without the will to make such sacrifices, what hope did humanity have? At least, that's what his father had said before he shipped out.

Soon the mag-rail came to a halt, and Deputy Springer knew it was time.

In less than ten minutes Springer and his men, along with the Einherjar, had left the relative safety of the mag-rail and descended into the sewers below. Apparently, the commanders of this task force were eager to avoid contact or even notice by the general population. Partly, he assumed, because they didn't want to complicate an already delicate military operation within civilian territory, though now that he'd spent several hours in their company he had another opinion.

The Einherjar were terrifying.

These armored men were clones of the warriors they used to be, having died and returned to life over and over in their seemingly endless war with the garm. They spoke only of war and tactics, and the banter of normal men was something they seemed to have forgotten. They seemed as alien to him as the garm, though at least these warriors appeared human. Perhaps that was what he found most disturbing, after all, was that they were not quite men, but something else.

War on two legs and death with a familiar face.

Deputy Springer fell in step with the rest of his deputies as they, along with the Einherjar, walked down the concrete steps that led into the tunnel system. His men were at the head of the procession of soldiers, as other deputies would be across this quadrant, leading other warriors into the tunnel system. The Einherjar were looking for something, a garm organism that they expected to attempt escape over conflict, and the plan was to encircle the beast and its brood before pulling the noose tight.

"When they come, stay behind us," Skald Omar said to the deputies as he followed close by, "Do not allow your pride to press you towards heroics better left to others. You can but die the once."

If the man's words were meant to be uplifting, Deputy Springer thought to himself, they were not. Yet again, these men were so used to fighting such terrors that even the thought of death was of little consequence. Springer tightened his grip on the sub-machine gun and continued sloshing through the murk and the muck, glad at least to have a weapon in his hands.

As Springer nodded at Skald Omar, the warrior's head suddenly rocked forward as a bolt round bashed into the back of his helmet. The skald stumbled and turned just in time fall face first into the muck. Another marine rushed to help him and the super-heated rounds of another salvo shattered his armor and blew out most of his mid-section. The other marines shouted and the deputy ducked as several marines opened fire upon the darkness, watching helplessly as another marine was gunned down by the unseen assailant.

He was about to rise when an explosion rocked the tunnels and everything devolved into bloody chaos.

Deputy Springer saw marines shooting in all directions, from the collapsed hole in the tunnel wall another warrior emerged. He was armored liked the Einherjar, and had the name Fagan stenciled upon his chest, but most of him was covered in gore and caked sewage, as if he'd been living and killing down here for a long time. This new warrior blasted a marine off his feet with short bursts from a compact pulse rifle, tossed what appeared to be a grenade into the formation of soldiers and everyone scattered.

The explosion knocked Deputy Springer to his knees. When he looked up, the enemy warrior was leveling a pulse rifle at his face. Before the enemy could squeeze the trigger Skald Omar, his helmet gone, leapt upon the enemy warrior. Their struggle brought them splashing and thrashing to the ground as both of them slid wicked looking blades, more like spikes really, out of sheathes, and began stabbing at each other.

Deputy Springer tried to get a clean shot, but he knew he would hit Omar. As he waited for an opening, another marine leapt into the fray. The new marine smashed the stock of his rifle into the back of the enemy warrior's head, and while the warrior was stunned the marine shoved him to the side wall of the tunnel and pinned him with a boot to the shoulder. The marine fired his pulse rifle twice, shattering the enemy warrior's armor and spraying the tunnel, himself, and Deputy Springer with gouts of smoldering blood and gore.

Springer got to his feet and wiped his eyes, taking in the sight of Omar still laying on the tunnel floor. His eyes were open and Springer could see where he'd been stabbed several times. The tunnels were still again, save for the sounds of wounded men. This pause in the violence was the calm before the storm.

He actually smelled them before he heard them, a rotting meat odor that wafted over him and nearly made him gag, even through his standard issue breather.

Then he heard them.

The scuttling sound of their claws on concrete and the clicking of mandibles matched only by the clatter of combat armor as the marines shouldered their way past the deputies to form a firing line.

When he saw them, their alien faces a horrendous blend of insect and reptile, it threatened to loosen his bowels.

He fired on them before he understood them. A ripper drone, if he recalled the briefing correctly, came screaming out of a pipe above the formation.

Springer's sub-machine gun roared in the darkness, the pulse rifles of the marines began to bark and spit death at the others. The range was close, and his spray of bullets tore the drone to pieces and gravity continued to bring it down. Springer leapt out of the way and splashed to the ground hard, as the corpse landed in the fetid water where he'd been standing. More drones dropped down from the ceiling while others charged the marine firing line.

He heard the marines shouting something about rapid evolution, but such was lost in the cacophony of violence that filled the tunnels. He watched with gut-churning horror as a drone slid down through a pipe so small he doubted a child could have come through there. As the beast landed on the ground its body rapidly expanded, as if the hardened chitin of the standard ripper drones had been replaced by a more flexible cartilage. That would certainly explain why neither the deputies nor the Einherjar noticed the flank attack at first.

Springer fired again, but his hands were shaking and his salvo did little but ricochet off the walls. The now fully expanded ripper drone snarled at him and charged. As Springer fumbled for another magazine, he cursed his fingers for not working faster, then he dropped the magazine in the dark water. He crouched to grab frantically for it, looking up in time to see the ripper drone live up to its name as it tore apart Deputy Watson with a flurry of claws and blades and teeth. His hands wrapped around the magazine and he slammed it into the slot, managing to rack the slide and cut loose on full-auto just as the creature was upon him.

The close-up fire riddled the monster with holes and sent it stumbling backwards, falling onto its back in the stinking water. Deputy Springer screamed as he kept firing, bearing down on the beast. Something had awoken inside him, and a primitive fury burned in his chest. He reloaded as fast as he could but saw that while he had managed to conduct himself, the majority of his deputies had not.

He watched as one of the garm organisms he'd learned was called a gorehound fired a bio-weapon at Deputy Lorne. Hundreds of tiny grubs flew through the half-light of the tunnel and pounded into the deputy's body. Those that did not splatter against her standard issue body armor chewed through her flesh and appeared to explode deep inside her. A marine blew the creature's head apart and then gestured at Springer.

"This way Deputy, we have to press on!" shouted the marine with the name Ajax on his chest, and Deputy Springer ran towards him, yelling for his men to follow.

As they rushed in to follow the marine down a side tunnel Deputy Springer looked back and to see that what had begun as a tight formation of marines had devolved into a chaotic free-for-all. The enemy was coming at them from all directions.

Springer swallowed hard and then turned to follow Ajax deeper into the tunnels.

DEATH AND DARKNESS

The marine never saw it coming.

He stalked his way down one of the many tunnels in the Tankrid underworld, the barrel of his pulse rifle still hot to the touch from furious use. The rest of his fire team lay dead in pieces somewhere behind him in the darkness. Fighting gorehounds face to face was indeed a messy affair, and the marine knew that it was by luck alone that he'd survived at all.

Communications were unreliable, and truth be told, the radio chatter was just a distraction at this point. The entire Einherjar front had devolved into a wild melee and it didn't seem like anyone knew what was going on. The marines were still getting used to being on the offensive, and fresh as he was in the role of aggressor, the marine knew they'd been drawn into a trap. The garm wanted them to come down here in full force, and waited until they were fully committed before attacking from all sides.

The strangeness of it was that the garm were just as bloodied by this fight as the marines, and if they were actually protecting a hive, this was the worst way to do so. The garm forces were just as smashed and disorganized as the marines. Where they should have been clustering together and protecting a central hive they were careening down the tunnels in a frenzy to find marine flesh. It made no sense.

So caught up in the madness of it, the marine did not notice the giant armored figure that slid upwards from the bottom of a sluice pit. Raw sewage ran down the monster's armor as it slowly stood to its full height. Movement to his left gave the marine cause to raise his rifle and follow it. In his sights he saw a wounded ripper drone limping down the tunnel, alone and berserk. It was dying, yet it came at him all the same. The marine lined up his shot and took the beast, yet before he could fully register his accomplishment a clawed hand gripped his helmet from above.

The hand wretched his face upwards to expose his throat, and another claw dug in between the seams in his armor. In seconds his esophagus was torn out and his veins sprayed arterial blood across the sewer walls. The armored figure let the marine's body fall to the ground, and then strode back down the passage from which the ripper drone had come. Soon the armored killer discovered evidence of the firefight that had left the drone wounded and alone.

Loki moved silently among the dead, his seven eyes taking in the sight of the slaughtered masses. He had known all along that it would come to this, but that foreknowledge brought him no comfort. Not unlike Odin himself, thought Loki as he picked his way over the ravaged corpses of marine and drone alike, who gained the awareness of all things. It brought the one-eyed god not a single measure of peace, Loki recalled as he knelt down and carefully observed the mandibles of a dead drone before slowly lifting them out of the punctured armor and flesh of a dead marine, and though it made the god Odin powerful, so too, did it make him the grimmest and most alone of his kind.

The wild uprising had done its job, and now the vast tunnel network had descended into bloody chaos. There were no battle lines now, only pockets of warriors fighting to survive against clutches of garm.

Loki was relieved not to have the burden of guiding the swarms upon his psychic shoulders. He now understood with perfect clarity just how great a task it was for the WarGarm to lead. Cut loose from the leash of his influence, the swarms of ripper drones and gorehounds rampaged through the underworld, their suicidal fury preventing the human forces from re-grouping, so focused were they on pure survival.

His keen senses warned him that several marines, a fire team, were moving down a tunnel close to the intersection ahead and Loki quickly thumbed the safety off his combo weapon. He reached up and grasped a pipe embedded into the ceiling and hefted himself upwards pressing flat against the ceiling. He used his powerful legs to hold himself in place, pushing against either end of the passage wall, using one hand to keep himself steady.

The Einherjar emerged from the tunnel and swept into the intersection, their armor covered in ichor and viscera from a previous conflict. Gorehounds by the stench of it. There were five of them in all, moving with tactical precision as they secured the intersection. The man nearest Loki looked up and saw the traitor who was partially hidden in the shadows. He raised his rifle, but before it was to his shoulder, Loki squeezed his own trigger, and spat several conventional rounds at the marine. The high velocity rounds would do little against the robust bodies of the garm, which was why they'd been replaced by the pulse rifles of the Einherjar. The rounds were, however, terribly effective in shattering the perpetually recycled combat armor of the marines.

The marine jerked backwards and fell with a splash into the knee-deep sewage at the bottom of the tunnel. For all their adaptations to combat against the garm, the marines had left themselves vulnerable to conventional weapons. No warrior could be perfectly suited for combat against all enemies, this much any man knew, and as the saviors of humanity, it had never entered their minds that they might have to battle their own.

The other marines fired on Loki's position, though he'd anticipated their counter-attack and let go of his hold on the walls. The warrior landed gracefully on the floor of the tunnel and drilled another marine with three tight bursts of fire from his combo weapon. As the marines adjusted their aim, the bolts from their weapons tore chunks of concrete and metal out of the walls, ceiling, and floor of the subterranean environment.

They were fast, each a consummate soldier, but they did not have the power of the garm, so as swiftly as they could adjust their aim, more easily was Loki able to evade their deadly salvos. The traitor leapt from the floor and drove a claw through the metal of a girder above so that he could twist his torso while swinging his legs around, bringing his weapon to bear as he avoided another burst of fire. This time, he pumped bolts from his pulse rifle into the half-light of the intersection. The first of the super-heated rounds crushed the marine's armor and the rounds that followed blew apart his left thigh.

Loki let go of the girder and fell to the ground as bolts ripped the girder to pieces above him, though of the two marines who yet stood, one had anticipated the maneuver. The marine pounded Loki's chest with a well-placed shot that sent the traitor slamming into the far wall. The traitor's reinforced armor was slagged, and his flesh burned as the molten remnants flowed in rivulets down his chest on either side of the ragged hole. Had he still been only Skald Thatcher he'd have been a dead man, though he was now Loki, and the wild fire of the garm burned in his DNA.

The traitor sprayed conventional rounds in a wide arc across the intersection, more to buy himself time to recover than to kill. Both of the remaining marines were knocked off of their feet by the blasts, though Loki's keen senses knew neither of them had sustained fatal injuries.

While one struggled with his wounds, the other marine thrashed to his feet and returned fire, but by then Loki was on the move again. The shooting marine did his best to track the enemy, but there was only a blur in the iron sights.

Loki smashed his leg into the side of the shooter, feeling the armor crack at the impact as his blow sent the marine soaring across the intersection. By the time his foot returned to the floor Loki had turned and shot the other wounded marine with his pulse rifle, the super-heated bolt making a red ruin of the warrior.

To his credit, the marine with the undoubtedly shattered ribcage was already on his feet and sliding his pistol out of its holster.

"Farewell, brave men," slurred Loki, his human vocal chords struggling to form the words that he'd grown accustomed to communicating with spoor and psychic vibration, before he blasted the wounded marine off his feet.

He paused to take a deep breath, filling his multi-chambered lungs with the scent of death and sewage. He reached out with his mind and found Hel's psychic presence waiting for him. The alpha garm was restless and eager for blood, though he knew she would not leave her clutch of eggs, as many had yet to hatch. The swarms had bought them time, though perhaps not yet enough.

"Withdraw to the egg chamber and hold that position," ordered Loki over the team channel, his voice giving sound to the words, though the communication itself was more psychic missive than anything. It was just as well considering the unreliable transmissions this far beneath the streets of Tankrid.

He knew that Ajax was down here with them, and could feel the hero's psychic searching wash over him like a wave. This time Loki chose not to obfuscate himself as he sped through the tunnels, his intimate knowledge of the layout enabling him to swiftly approach the chamber, and instead made his psychic presence radiate with malevolent challenge.

Now that they'd divided the marine advance, Ajax would not be at the head of an army, but most likely a much smaller force. A manageable number of foes was ideal for what was to come next.

Loki entered the chamber within minutes, having taken a shortcut that the ripper drones had dutifully bored through the raw earth. Once he'd exited the shortcut he lifted a concussion charge from his utility belt and twisted the top after setting the dial for five seconds. He leaned back into the opening and pitched it far back down the makeshift tunnel. Moments later the dull thud of the explosion shook the raw passage and brought it collapsing in on itself. It would not do for errant marines or deputies to come crawling out of there at an inopportune moment.

Loki turned and saw that of his skalds, only four had heeded his call, Unferth among them. The skald leader strode up to Loki and handed the traitor two bloody torcs, which the traitor took and hung on his bandolier, ever did it grow heavier. Loki then turned and cast his gaze across the chamber, taking note that even now some of the eggs were hatching.

"The first clutch has already been secured aboard the *Angrboda*," reported Unferth, anticipating his master's question. "How long we must wait for the next, remains to be seen."

"If the Einherjar come any closer, Hel will force them to emerge," said Loki, knowing that like moths and butterflies these garm broodlings needed to hatch on their own. "Without the natural struggle they'll be too undeveloped, and as we have learned, the intellect comes only with maturity. A premature brood would be good for a last stand but futile in the face of our great work."

Loki looked at his men as he considered his options, made his choice, and then spoke.

"The Einherjar are as strong as they've ever been, much as we have accomplished, they have fought through what defenses and distractions we could mount. We will have to make do with the broodlings we have.

Cigovax and Unferth, secure the garm whelk, get them aboard and prep the ship for hard burn," ordered Loki. The traitor turned to the remaining two. "Karn and Hastur, roll out the incendiary canisters and get them into position."

"What about you, sir?" asked Unferth as he slowly lifted one of the garm whelks out of the fetid pool.

"It is high time Ajax and I crossed swords," growled Loki as he ejected his half-spent magazine and replaced it with a fresh one.

THE ALL CHANGE

Ajax fought to keep his hands steady as he led the fire team through the maddening system of tunnels. His mind was completely open, and he gritted his teeth with the effort of maintaining his forward momentum despite the crushing presence of Hel.

That wasn't the only thing weighing down on him. For the first time, there was a second presence with them in the underworld. It was at once familiar and alien, like a half-remembered resurrection dream, and it distinctly reminded him of Grendel. If psychic emanations could leave a taste in the back of a man's throat then this would be not unlike the sharp copper of blood.

The Hive Mind was getting stronger, the force of it squeezing his mind and what felt like his very soul as he careened through the flickering shadows of the tunnel network. Now that he was so close to the source, and far too exhausted to close himself off to it, he began to detect subtleties he'd not yet encountered, that he suspected had been there all along.

Hel wasn't the Hive Mind, it was an alpha garm, and this other presence, the familiar one, wasn't the Hive Mind either. Nor were the multitudes of ripper drones and gorehounds that continued to rampage through the tunnels without stratagem now that their WarGarm had been slain.

They were all the Hive Mind.

Such a simple concept to grasp, yet so unfathomable in the experience of it.

It felt, to Ajax, that if he grasped at the Hive Mind too hard, not only would it fade before his awareness, but he would risk slipping into the murky depths of the garm collective unconsciousness.

The realization made him wish, fervently, that Skald Omar or Jarl Mahora also stood with him in this moment, but they, like so many others, were lost to him now.

He recalled the sight of the traitorous skald Fagan driving his trench spike into Omar and he, too, shook with the impact of that blow. It was as if the entire world Ajax had built around himself had collapsed in that single moment.

The traitor skald's blood was still wet upon him, a cruel reminder of an unthinkable betrayal. Up was down, down was sideways, and it was all inside out.

"We are close now," Ajax whispered over the team channel, trusting that the deputies would keep quiet and just follow the marines without question.

"Lead on, Bloodhound," said Hart flatly, in his usual monotone, his sniper rifle slung across his back and a scavenged pulse rifle held at the ready.

Yao nodded, as did Silas, and they kept pace with Ajax as the marine held his rifle before him, the mounted light illuminating a two-way intersection. When he came to the intersection, Ajax felt himself pulled down one end of the tunnel, but was determined to open the hatch that lay ahead. He signaled for Yao and Rama to take either end, and as they popped it open, Ajax and Hart rushed in ready for anything.

Almost anything, but his eyes were met, not with a horrible garm hive, but with a modest chamber seemingly occupied by a human. There was a small table, a sleeping mat, and what appeared to be an incense burner set in the center of the chamber. The presence of the alien other was strong here, as if whatever it was, had left behind a psychic spoor that Ajax could taste.

It was Hart who noticed the hands first.

"Ajax, take heed," warned the skald sniper as he gestured with the muzzle of his weapon. "Again, the sign of Tyr is set before us."

Ajax followed with his eyes and stifled a groan as he saw nine hands messily bolted into the concrete wall above the modest sleeping mat.

They were old, the blood that seeped from them having dried in streaks along the wall.

They stood in silence for a moment, until Deputy Springer stepped forward and pointed to one with a small circular tattoo on the thumb.

"That belongs to Deputy Stratton. A family crest, he was so proud of that thing, I'd recognize it anywhere," he rasped, the stinking air and strain of battle having made him rather hoarse. "Who would do this to a man?"

"The trophy taker is here then," said Yao, his voice and body trembling with rage, a reminder that he struggled daily with the black, even more than Ajax. "Somewhere in the dark."

"I suspect the trophy taker has always been near us," said Hart, drawing looks from the others. "I suspect the narrative has been compromised since Heorot."

Before he could properly respond, Ajax was suddenly overcome with the sensation of a new psychic presence in his mental landscape, something raw and young, though possessed of much tenacity and hunger. It was as if one moment he had achieved a sort of equilibrium with the dueling presences in his psychic mindscape, then all of a sudden, many more sparks exploded from the flame, nearly overwhelming him. The psychic sensation was complemented by a distinct tearing sound that filled the passageway outside. Everyone had their guns up in an instant, and then looked at Ajax for orders.

Ajax said nothing, but looked at his Einherjar comrades with steel in his eyes and turned to leave the chamber. Once back into the intersection, he started making his way down the passage.

Coming up the opposite way they saw several mounted lights that revealed themselves to be Jorah and another marine from Gorgon Company. They said nothing, but as Ajax and Hart pressed forward they fell in line just after Yao and Silas, leaving the deputies to bring up the rear.

As the rest of the group fell in behind him, Ajax's mounted light reflected against the glistening resin that he recognized as a garm secretion. The massive archway led into darkness, so the marine slipped a flare out of his utility belt. The other two marines did the same.

Ajax popped the flare and tossed it into the chamber as he slammed his shoulder into the wall on the left side of the entrance. Yao tossed his as he took the right, and Silas rushed up the middle to throw his deeper into the chamber. As soon as they threw the flares, the three marines formed a firing line and advanced as Hart, Jorah, and the other Gorgon marine backed them up. Deputy Springer and his two men followed, their sub-machine guns at the ready.

The combined light of the flares glinted off polished black eyes, and the marines were met with a sight none of them could have anticipated.

A garm monstrosity that could only be Hel squatted in the center of the chamber, surrounded by multitudes of eggs that were spread out across the massive room. She had the look of a WarGarm, but warped and twisted to resemble something like an arachnid. In the flickering red light of the flares, Ajax could see that the chamber was covered in eggs. The alpha garm screamed and they all began to quiver violently.

Before Ajax's horrified gaze, one of the eggs split open and the shuddering, naked form of a man arose from the shards.

The marines and deputies were paralyzed by what they saw, nothing, in all their years at war, even with the oddities of recent conflicts with Grendel and the alpha garm, could equal the nightmare laid before them.

As birthing fluids ran down the man's body, he turned to face the intruders and the deputies fell to their hands and knees vomiting.

The man looked normal enough at first glance, then his eyes opened to reveal the same polished black of Hel, of the ripper drones, of the garm. The skin on his face suddenly shifted, tearing in several places, sliding back across his face to partially reveal a hideous garm beneath. It had the cockroach meets reptile facial traits shared by all organisms of the swarm, though it looked far too human for Ajax to keep himself from screaming.

The man's body followed his face and parts of his human facade tore and receded to unleash the terrible claws and scything blades that the Einherjar knew all too well. It lent its inhuman voice to the screams coming from the marines and charged.

As it ran towards them, dozens more eggs split apart and slime covered, naked men and women-looking creatures stood erect.

Somewhere in the half-light Hart shouted for the marines to open fire.

Ajax's mind was suddenly overwhelmed with rage. There was a fury surging in him that could not be held in check, and he charged the abomination as he fired from the hip.

The marine's first round blew out the creature's mid-section. The second round knocked it off its feet to send it tumbling backwards onto the floor.

Another beast tore its way out of an egg as Hel continued her keening, and Ajax didn't hesitate to shove the barrel of his pulse rifle under the naked woman's chin and reduce her head to a steaming stump.

Yao was suddenly at his side, and Ajax could see that Yao was gone. The sight of the humanoid garm, the presence of Hel, and the sudden death of Omar at the hands of a betrayal they still could not understand had finally pushed him over the edge.

The marine held his pistol in one hand and his trench spike in the other as he leapt into the thick of the humanoid garm, slaughtering them as they emerged from their eggs. Such was the potency of Yao's sudden blackout that it shocked Ajax back to sanity. He knelt, bringing his rifle to his shoulder. He'd rushed in, and was downrange from his comrades, so knew he had to make himself the smallest target possible to avoid friendly fire while still conducting himself effectively.

Yao was a whirlwind of carnage, and in the brief respite from enemy attention, Ajax risked a look back. Behind him, the other marines were falling back, laying down methodical bursts of fire with a cold discipline that would have made the All-Father proud indeed. The marines were screaming as they fired, though they were managing to keep their shooting form in top condition. Four determined marines in a target rich environment were a sight to behold.

The deputies were struggling to their feet, lacking the mental and physical constitution of the Einherjar, but doing what they could in the face of cosmic terror. In truth it was a testament to their dedication that the deputies hadn't cut and run after the first swarm came raging out of the darkness. More of the sickening humanoid garm were rushing the deputies. Just in time, Ajax saw Deputy Springer paste one with his sub-machine gun.

Ajax felt something moving up on his flank, and he turned muzzle first to face a humanoid garm as it pounced upon him. His pulse rifle kept its teeth from clamping down on his face, but as he pulled the trigger two tiny fangs protruded suddenly from inside the beast's maw. Its throat constricted as the marine blew a massive hole through its torso and a thick cloud of what Ajax presumed were spores temporarily obscured his vision.

Ajax rolled and brought his rifle in, giving him the chance to smash the stock of the rifle into the dying creature's jaw and send it sprawling. He'd cranked the filter of his helmet to its max setting, and was thankful for that. The marine rolled onto his back and pointed his rifle upwards.

To his surprise Hel had not moved, and he noticed that she was still attached to a massive undulating sack. As the firefight continued Ajax saw that Hel was still laying eggs.

She was single-minded in her task, perhaps some part of her garm instinct giving her an intense focus on her work and an implicit trust in her offspring to protect the hive. Ajax snapped his rifle to his shoulder and unleashed three quick bursts of fire at the alpha garm, taking deep satisfaction in the great chunks of burning flesh and chitin his attack ripped from Hel's abdomen.

He cast about for Yao and saw the marine's ravaged body strewn across the chamber, his rage only having carried him so far before his pistol ran dry, and his spike was no match against the scything blades of the garm.

"*Meat!*" screamed Deputy Springer as he tackled Ajax to the ground.

Ajax lost his grip on the pulse rifle and it clattered across the gore-slick floor. The deputy gripped Ajax by the helmet and smashed the marine's face into the concrete floor. Like the other ragmen that Ajax had encountered over his long tour of duty, ragman Springer was using every last ounce of strength in his body, caring little for torn muscles or broken bones. Ajax reeled from the second blow and tried to roll over to grapple with the deputy. Quite unlike the usual ragmen, the deputy retained an understanding of how to fight. Ajax managed to get the deputy into an arm bar, but instead of yielding, the deputy allowed the marine to snap his arm at the elbow.

The sacrifice of his arm allowed the deputy to let go of Ajax with his other hand and yank his short pistol out of its holster.

Ragmen did not use guns.

The thought played over and over in the marine's mind as he felt the first shot slam into his armor and crack it. The deputy apparently lost patience and stood up for a cleaner shot, moving the pistol up to point it at Ajax's head. Just as he started to squeeze the trigger, the deputy's chest exploded.

Ajax scurried out from under the remains of the deputy and yanked his own sidearm out of its holster. He saw Hart kneel to vent his pulse rifle. The deputies were both dead on the floor, one of them with the rictus smile that marked him as having become a ragman. Silas was limping with the help of Jorah, and the other Gorgon marine looked to have been torn apart by blade and claw.

Ajax struggled to his feet as the other marines fought their way to him. He could see that the humanoid garm had lost their initial advantage in numbers, as most of their brood had now been slain. He picked up his pulse rifle, slapped in a fresh magazine, joining his comrades in methodically pulping Hel's seemingly fragile body. They vented the heat from their rifles and then began slaughtering the humanoids as they hatched. It was a cold kind of fury, and what had begun as a battle had become an execution. The marines were fine with that, and did their work with precision and gusto.

Silas was suddenly thrown backwards as a shot rang out from above them. More shots followed as Silas stumbled, and in seconds his body was riddled with bullets.

Ajax, Hart, and Jorah swept their guns upwards and gasped as they saw a gigantic armored figure leaping down from a hatch far above.

Ajax recognized much of the armor as that of a skald but it had been heavily modified and he could see seven glowing red oculars in the creature's helmet. The enemy's weapon had been modified as well, impossibly toggling between the tiny projectiles of conventional ammunition and the caseless bolts of carbon used in the pulse rifles.

The skald that wasn't a skald at all, ran horizontally across the wall, digging a clawed hand into the concrete to slow its descent, carving great gouts into the wall itself.

"The trophy taker," observed Hart, the tone of his voice giving the impression that he was speaking to himself more than to the others. He raised his rifle and returned fire, tracking the descending hostile with bolts that got closer and closer to hitting the mark.

The marines scrambled for cover as they fired, the armored hostile moving impossibly fast as it continued downwards. The enemy unleashed a salvo of rounds that forced Ajax to hurl himself behind a clutch of hatched eggs. The spray of conventional small arms fire chewed through the thick hide of the eggs and showered Ajax with the ichor of garm afterbirth. The marine stayed low and scampered around in a wide circle to bring himself adjacent to Hel's bulbous corpse.

As Jorah and Hart continued the shootout with the armored hostile, Ajax looked to his left, just beyond the body of Hel. Even in death, her body was ejecting eggs onto the slick floor of the disgusting chamber.

He was awestruck at the sheer relentlessness of the garm organisms. It seemed that no matter what nightmares he experienced, there was always a fresh and terrible example of the swarm's might. Though dead, the alpha garm yet brought forth life, and Ajax found himself chilled to the core by the sight of it.

The shooting intensified and Ajax shook himself into action, knowing he had to get back into the fight. He raised himself to a crouching position and pulled the stock of his pulse rifle tight into his shoulder. Ajax looked down his iron sights and saw that the armored hostile had reached the ground. He snapped off a shot at the enemy, but it was moving too quickly and his bolt went wide. Ajax rushed to meet the hostile, trying to put himself in the creature's path as it sprinted nimbly through the shattered remains of the humanoid garm and the hatched eggs.

Hart and Jorah, the latter of which was using only his pistol, as his right arm had been blown off at the elbow, saw Ajax make his play and lent their firepower to driving the armored hostile into his field of fire.

At first it seemed like it would work, as the fiend exchanged salvos with the two marines counter-attacking him. Just as Ajax sighted in on the armored monster it leapt low and streaked underneath his burst of deadly fire. The beast's double-jointed legs had been gathered beneath it and he'd not realized it could pounce from a sprint, and before Ajax could react the creature's shoulder drove into his mid-section.

The beast was large and powerful, and Ajax felt his breath leave him as he lost the grip on his rifle and soared backwards to slam wetly into a clutch of eggs. He'd fallen on his back, and witnessed the armored creature twist its arm around and fire upon the marines trying to flank it. Jorah grunted and was picked up off his feet by a solid bolt to the chest in a spray of blood and broken armor as the hostile suddenly dug its feet into the ground and halted its own momentum.

Ajax pushed himself to his feet and drew his pistol, only to have the monster lash out with it the claws of its armored foot and slice through his hand and the pistol. The marine cursed in frustration and pain as his pistol clattered to the ground in pieces, followed by three of his own severed fingers. Before he could recover, the beast smashed an elbow into the side of his helmet and sent him crashing to the ground once more.

The marine's vision swam from the impact, though he could partially make out Hart, fearless as ever, appear from the shadows and attack the creature. The skald sniper fired a round straight into the beast's helmeted face, and two of the seven oculars went dark. The creature reeled from the hit and Hart pumped more rounds at it. They were deflected by the elevated shoulder pieces that protected its head, but the sniper had an opening. He leapt towards the beast, his trench spike flashing, and buried it in the hole already scored in the creature's armored chest. It must have fought other marines before attacking them, Ajax realized as he struggled to rise to his knees.

The beast screamed in pain and rage, and dropped its rifle so that it could deflect Hart's pistol. In a blur of motion, the creature lashed out at the warrior with clawed hands. Hart did his best to defend himself with the trench spike, but the creature was far too fast for him. The armored attacker rent Hart to bloody ribbons with a furious tempest of blows, and by the time Ajax got to his feet with his own trench spike at the ready, his comrade was very dead.

Ajax attempted to backstab the creature as it concentrated on tearing the last bit of life from Hart's body. It must have felt him coming, as it easily deflected his blow and grasped him by the throat, squeezing so hard he heard the armor around his neck crack beneath its alien hands. With its other clawed hand it wrenched the helmet from Ajax's head, and its remaining five oculars transfixed him with their burning gaze.

"Ajax," rasped a voice from beneath the helmet, the words reaching the marine's ears a moment after they registered in his mind.

The marine said nothing as he flailed with arms and legs against the nightmare before him, his fists doing little to break the armored thing's grip upon him. It held him aloft with ease, and though he attempted to kick the thing he could not reach it. His oxygen was running out, and only a few seconds into the ordeal, he was already seeing stars begin to sparkle in his vision, a sure sign that he would soon be unconscious.

Something about the thing was familiar, and though he knew with certainty that this was the other presence he'd felt in the tunnels, Ajax could not place who or what this thing might be. It had Einherjar armor and weapons, though all modified beyond anything within regulation. Also it had the stink of the garm upon it, and the psychic waves buffeted against him with tremendous force.

It felt to Ajax as if a hurricane held him in its grasp, such was the sheer power of the mind that bore down on him.

"The *Angrboda* bore me three children, marine. Beautiful as they were terrible before they met with your blades and your guns. Indeed they were titans of the swarm, and the Einherjar have more than earned a place in Valhalla by the slaying of them," hissed the armored creature as it squeezed Ajax even harder.

Ajax watched in horror as with its other hand the beast unfastened the clamps on its helmet, and as the seals broke it lifted the visor to reveal a hideously twisted visage beneath. Indeed, the garm abomination had seven eyes, and wide hinged jaws that appeared to be folded together so that the face could fit inside the confines of the helmet. Past all of the garm traits, it was the sickening realization of who he looked upon that made Ajax's blood freeze.

"*Skald Thatcher*," gasped Ajax, using what little strength he had left to spit the words out like a curse.

"Something more. Something worse." said Loki, in a voice that sounded like stale meat scraped against sandpaper, "And nothing at all."

The creature throttled Ajax a moment longer in silence, and once the marine's struggle had all but left him, the beast held him close to its hideous face.

"Humanity has lost its way, so too, has the extinction fleet. Two houses, both alike in dignity, and neither deserving of a throne," whispered Loki, his vocal chords warping the words to make them sound all the more alien. "This war must end, Ajax. It is time you forget what you've seen here. Goodbye, marine."

"I thought you were a hero," spoke Ajax, his voice a ragged whisper as he fought to stay conscious.

"Hero is another word for a dead man," growled Loki, before opening his jaws wide and snapping them shut across the marine's face.

The powerful mandibles drove the rows of wicked teeth through the marine's skull, and the last thing Ajax experienced before total darkness was the putrid breath of the monster that slew him.

SCORCHED EARTH

Jarl Mahora knelt down and ran his finger over the close up shot of the ashen sludge that coated the inside of the massive chamber. The combat footage played on a small tablet he held in his rough hands as he sat alone in the briefing room. He watched as several fire teams swept through the chamber, their armor protecting them from the ambient heat that lingered.

The hardened veteran looked at the twisted remains of a multitude of bodies, each of them burned down to little more than clumps of carbon slag. There would be no telling what was marine and what was garm in this mess, the fire having burned so hot that the concrete itself had run in rivulets only to reharden, giving the entire room the appearance of having been made of melted and cooled wax.

"M3 incendiary canisters," said Skald Wallace as he strode into the room carrying a small plastic case, with Idris, the medicae, entering a few steps behind him. "Every Prax gunship has a standard load-out of eight. I suspect no less than four were deployed here, given the blast points."

"We should have seen this coming," growled Mahora as he tossed the tablet onto the table at the center of the room and stood to his full height to show respect to the skald with a curt nod, while at attention. "It was only going to be a matter of time before the garm turned us against our own."

"We have known about the rogue skald element for some time now, and given that they escaped with Grendel's remains, we have suspected their involvement in the various alpha garm run to ground by your man, Ajax," admitted Skald Wallace as he nodded back and then held up a hand to silence Mahora's predicable angry response. "Save it. We took a calculated risk by not making infantry forces aware. It seemed a pointless morale risk."

"And now?" spat Mahora as he sat back down and rubbed his temples, the veteran marine was feeling the years suddenly and more powerfully than ever before. "The marines look up to your skalds, because most of them are living legends. To see your battle brothers slain by your idols, to fill your iron sights with the bodies of other Einherjar who seem to fight on the side of the garm, that is a heavy thing, Wallace."

"There is a deep madness at work here, Jarl," observed Wallace as he set the case onto the table and opened it to produce a warped and melted torc. "I suspect those incendiaries had a two-fold purpose. One to wipe out all evidence of whatever foul deeds were afoot here, the second to forever destroy the memory of what your marines encountered there."

Idris took the torc from Wallace and walked it over to Jarl Mahora. The veteran turned the torc over and over in his hands, as if he could not believe the malevolence and cunning it represented on the part of the enemy. He recognized the torc, and it had belonged to marine Ajax.

They had salvaged the torc of Ajax when he'd fought Jormungandr and died shortly after, and so the memories of that life lived were saved and laid into the new body they'd grown for the marine's mind. Since then Ajax had survived against Fenrir and fought his way into this pit of darkness. With the torc destroyed now, not only would Ajax resurrect without the memory of his time on the forest moon, but he would not be able to give any intelligence on whatever it was he'd experienced down here. The same went for Silas, of Hydra Company, Jorah and Tamsen, of Gorgon Company, and even the nearly impossible to kill Hart, of the skalds. Whatever these men had seen down here was forever lost, and each man would return to life with memories only up to the last time his torc was uploaded.

"The traitors knew how to negate the torcs and cover their tracks with a single blow," breathed Jarl Mahora as the full gravity of what happened finally crashed down upon him.

"There's more," announced Idris, his own expression grave.

"Spit it out, man," snapped Mahora as he continued to look at the torc, as if the harder he stared at it the more he would understand the full extent of what had happened.

"The men who died in that room have all emerged from the body forge, without the memories of their encounter, though otherwise whole," said Idris before pausing, he looked back at Wallace, who nodded, and then back to Mahora, "Except for Ajax."

"What?" asked Mahora as he let the torc drop onto the table. "Is there a problem?"

"Physically, he has resurrected and is in the green," stated Idris, clearly uncomfortable as he delivered the news, "Though he remains in a vegetative state. Not quite like the victims of Grendel, nothing so violent, as he remains alive."

"For all intents and purposes, he has been taken off the board," said Skald Wallace, his voice hard.

"Have you euthanized him and attempted a second resurrection?" asked Jarl Mahora, his usual gruff demeanor seeming more beaten down as the conversation progressed. "Perhaps there was an error in the body forge itself."

"We have made this attempt three times, jarl. Something happened to him down there, and I have not been able to facilitate a full recovery," said Idris as he stood and put his hand on Mahora's shoulder. "I am sorry sir. The Bloodhound is gone."

"Many among us would say Beowulf is gone," said Skald Wallace as he stood once more and made to leave, "Even as the dragon returns to these lands. Bifrost is reporting swarms on the approach, and without our tracker it is time the task force returns to the front."

Skald Wallace exited the briefing room and let the door close behind him. Idris stayed a few moments longer, sitting in silence with the grizzled jarl before standing to leave.

"Ajax is gone," breathed Jarl Mahora as he looked down once more at the warped torc on the table before him, "They've found yet another way to rob us of our best."

"The garm adapt, do they not?" asked Idris, a grim smile playing across his face.

Upon hearing the familiar colloquialism, Mahora's melancholy was swept away by a grieving fury, and he stood up to activate the three-dimensional display at the center of the table. He toggled the images until he brought up the Bifrost, and then zoomed out until he was able to see the star fortress set against a looming mass of unidentified objects moving with speed towards it. They were weeks away, though time would seem short when it came to preparing for the sort of war that a garm swarm would bring with it.

"Marines overcome," snarled Mahora as he began his preparations for the coming battle.

Idris watched the man for a short time, and then left the room. He walked down several passageways and eventually entered the body forge.

While multitudes of other marines were in the process of being resurrected, attended by several of the lower ranking specialists, Idris walked over to stand next to the still body of Ajax. He gently leaned in and removed the brand new torc affixed to the marine's neck. Idris looked down at the man, this long-suffering marine, and typed a series of commands into the display next to the marine's forge.

Idris turned and walked to a small shelf, removing a hard, black case. Inside there were multitude of torcs. He held up the one that had belonged to Skald Thatcher, or more accurately the counterfeit he'd left in its place. He let the torc fall back onto the pile and then added the one he'd removed from Ajax. It made a clanking sound as it fell onto the pile.

Idris closed the case and returned it to the shelf as the console next to Ajax to begin executing its euthanasia protocols.

THE CENTER CANNOT HOLD

Loki stood in his own briefing room aboard the Angrboda and looked at a model of the vast expanse of human civilization. Each planet, moon, colony, and space station was present in the display before him. There were so many it looked as if there was a swarm of fireflies buzzing in front of the traitor's monstrous face.

The taste of Ajax was still in his mouth, though the brains of the marine he'd devoured had long been digested. The memories bubbled in a thick stew just beneath Loki's conscious awareness. One, in particular, continued to rise, despite his best efforts at keeping it down, the crisp recollection of Rowan, the long dead wife of the marine whose life he had ingested. It was difficult to push her away, as her presence always triggered yet more memories of his own Ariana, and it was all Loki could do to keep such things from overwhelming him.

He took a deep breath and focused his mind, for a time casting away the thoughts of lost love, and set himself to the task at hand. He moved his clawed finger up and zoomed in on a specific quadrant of the universe, then zoomed deeper still to bring up the view of a single human world. It was heavily populated, containing several mega-cities, and served as a trade hub for several massive systems.

It was perfect for the work ahead. Loki keyed in the coordinates and the crew of the Angrboda set a course. Loki deactivated the display and walked the short distance down a passageway from the briefing room to the command bridge. There he was met by Unferth, who stood just above and behind the pilot and gunnery crew.

"Common men are tossed into mass graves or left on the field for crows. Better to be a foe so hated your corpse is paraded like a trophy and hung high enough for the gods themselves to take notice," rasped Loki as he came to stand beside Unferth, the twisted being towering over the skald thanks to the garm cells that had long since made him into something less than human and more than garm.

"The mission, sir?" asked Unferth.

"Ragnarok"

Don't miss out!

Visit the website below and you can sign up to receive emails whenever Sean-Michael Argo publishes a new book. There's no charge and no obligation.

https://books2read.com/r/B-A-KCOJ-TJANC

Connecting independent readers to independent writers.

Also by Sean-Michael Argo

Extinction Fleet
Space Marine Loki
Space Marine Ajax

Starwing Elite
Attack Ships
Alpha Lance

Standalone
War Machines
DinoMechs: Battle Force Jurassic

Milton Keynes UK
Ingram Content Group UK Ltd.
UKHW040639040923
428018UK00001B/95